The Harp &

by

Frank Gilfeather

For Sharron, to whom I owe so much.

And for Paul, Lucy, Steven and Kathryn.

INTRODUCTION

The Industrial Revolution brought about factory weaving as the handloom system disappeared.

This was a boom time for the jute industry and, with housing needed for mill workers, tenement buildings sprang up all across Dundee.

The influx of Irish workers influenced the city's Lochee area where they even had their own little community, known as Tipperary.

By then, Lochee had distinctive and prominent landmarks; Cox's Stack, the towering chimney which was the centrepiece of the Camperdown Works mill and dominated the district, and St Mary's RC Church, designed by Joseph Hansom, the inventor of the hansom cab and the architect of a large number of public buildings, principally churches, throughout Britain.

It wasn't until the 19th century that this little town was enveloped by Dundee, though even to this day, ask someone from the area where they come from and they will invariably answer 'Lochee' rather than 'Dundee'.

The outbreak of World War II in 1939 brought with it the realisation that life would never be the same again. In came rationing of food, clothing and petrol and many of Dundee's schoolchildren were evacuated.

Sport at the highest level, including football, was suspended because large crowds would have been an easy target for German bombers.

Junior football teams, however, continued to participate, with two rival clubs – Lochee Harp and Dundee Violet – whose grounds were close, vying for superiority.

The Harp, as they are known, was formed in 1904 by local priests and some of the congregation of St Mary's Church as an Irish Catholic team.

The Violet was born as a breakaway from Hillbank FC in the 1880s and the club was to progress in dramatic fashion winning a raft of league titles in the 1920s and 1930s.

But their proudest moment came in the 1928-29 season when the team won the Scottish Junior Cup.

They beat the Harp in the opening round, a tie that sparked so much interest it was staged at Dundee FC's Dens Park to accommodate a large crowd. The 'Pansies' – Violet's nickname – won 2-1.

Denny Hibs were their opponents in the final at Tynecastle, Edinburgh, but following a 2-0 win for the Dundee outfit, it was discovered they had fielded in ineligible player and the game had to be replayed.

It ended with a 2-2 scoreline and a second replay took place at Dens Park where the local team emerged triumphant, winning 4-0 before 10,000 supporters of both sides.

1

May 2, 1941.

He was cold, weary, crumpled and dishevelled. Through the fading light and the drizzle, he peered at his watch only to discover that at some point during a journey fraught with difficulties it had broken, its face cracked and one of the hands dislodged and rattling about under the glass.

He guessed it must have been around ten o'clock, maybe later. The faint signs of the early May sunset and the fading soft gold he'd glimpsed tucked behind the broken clouds as he exited Tay Bridge Railway Station, must have been about an hour earlier when he took the first steps of his three-mile trek towards home.

Frank McGarrity's body was stiff, sore, pounded, as if he'd been tied down on his back of the bogey of a tractor driven over hundreds of miles of rocky farm tracks.

This is how a bruised and battered two-ton Tony Galento must have felt when Joe Louis slaughtered him in their world heavyweight championship fight the previous summer, he thought.

He stretched his arms sideways and bent backwards in a bid to ease the aches and pains in his bones and loosen his beat-up muscles after a disagreeable and often harrowing sojourn; five hundred or more punishing miles on the hard floors of a series of goods trains and trucks that rattled and zigzagged their way across the country.

The spring night-time temperature had not been too unkind during this hell of a trip. He'd experienced far worse during those short winter days and long, cold, miserable and worrying nights in France where he wondered when death would visit.

The problems of World War II, he told himself, had merely confirmed what, in his conceit, he had always believed - that he was tough mentally and physically; that the person he looked at in the mirror every morning was, indeed, a hard man.

He welcomed the evening air as the sun sank lower. The wispy rain dampened his dark, ruffled hair and moistened his Pioneer Corps tunic, dirty, torn and grubby from his torturous odyssey. But he wasn't one to care about the property of the army. He held it and all it stood for in utter contempt. There was a burning resentment, too, at having to do his duty for King and country. Sure, he had signed-up, but it was for the money, pure and simple, and, anyway, he knew that the recruiting sergeants would have come knocking on his door had he failed to put pen to paper as a new member of His Majesty's armed forces as additional soldiers, sailors and airmen were rounded-up.

McGarrity turned off the High Street opposite the red-stone public library and walked a few paces along Marshall Street before staring down at the two decaying rows of buildings at the foot of St Ann Street. Welcome back to Tipperary.

His heart skipped a few beats. His body inexplicably felt warmer and memories of his childhood danced around his mind; playing football on traffic-free roads, kicking a can around the streets to stave off boredom, trying to spook the placid, lumbering cart horses that pulled tons of jute bales from Dundee's busy harbour through the streets to the city's plethora of jute mills.

A semblance of a smile creased his fatigued face as he remembered those occasions when, still in short trousers, he would be sent on a mission to extricate his father from one of Lochee's many bars as the McGarrity matriarch called time on her husband's curfew.

This place was still home. It was somewhere his presence was not expected, but where he desperately wanted to be.

Casa McGarrity was a cramped two-roomed, dank and dingy tenement flat. The toilet, sited on the right-hand side at the top of fifteen exterior stone stairs, was the communal cludgie for the use of his family and three other households in the chilly, inhospitable and crumbling building. Water poured from leaky pipes like a stream that had no end.

Frank sorted his clothing and smiled to himself as he thought of his upbringing; ablutions in the house's multi-use sink, and a weekly bath, taken in a tin contraption in which the occupants would fit into it by curling-up like Harry Houdini preparing for one of his famous escapology stunts. The use of a proper bath was the douche domain of toffs. This was poverty in the raw in 1940s Britain, as it had been for previous generations.

The McGarrity dwelling was at 13a Atholl Street, opposite a similar building where his parents had raised him and three siblings.

It was two years since he'd been in Tipperary, not the landlocked rural county in Ireland, home to mountains, rivers, loughs, farmland and fresh air, but a ghetto of incomers trying desperately to retain their dignity in such unpleasant circumstances and surroundings.

Instead, this was Lochee, an area of Dundee where immigrants from the Emerald Isle - Donegal, Derry, Monaghan, Sligo and Tyrone - had settled from the mid-19th century, attracted by work in the burgeoning jute industry that had at its centre the giant mill owned by the wealthy Cox family and established a hundred years earlier by brothers James, William, Thomas and George and still run by their offspring. The Cox dynasty was influential and powerful at home and abroad.

Many of those early pioneer workers gravitated towards Lochee, with Tipperary its beating heart. They had come from those Irish counties where linen and yarn were produced and therefore knew the textiles industry and the skills required in this city by the River Tay.

And, as many had come from Tipperary, the county in the province of Munster, the name was given to this one-street barrio with its two hundred and fifty inadequate homes where space was at a premium.

Over the years many more Irish men and women and their families had made their way to Lochee, in the city of jute, jam and journalism. In time, the population of this mainly Catholic community was bolstered by Glaswegian and Glasgow-Irish waifs and strays, desperate for employment and a roof over their heads.

Like many of his contemporaries, McGarrity was the product of parents whose own mothers and fathers were Irish, while there were countless neighbours in this settlement who had been drawn to the jute mills from all over Scotland by the lure of work, principally for women; spinners and weavers.

Less than a year earlier, Frank had been up to his knees in mud, blood and bodies. Bullets and shells whistled past his head at Dunkirk. His focus for the moment, though, was the here and now. In a few minutes, his aching feet would climb that exterior stone staircase to the door of 13a and the warm embrace of his wife Bridget.

In the dimming light, he walked down the sloping street past a rough and bumpy piece of ground, known as Maloney's Park, to his left. He allowed his mind to turn to the life he had left behind when he joined the Pioneer Corps for what he thought would be a short spell.

2

She was a widow who occupied No.13b across the landing from Bridget McGarrity and had kept her neighbour company for an hour as the sun began to fall to the west, towards Perth. She had the lined face and gravel voice of someone who smoked too many Woodbines, which she did. It was her only vice, she used to say. And, if fags weren't available, she would have managed well enough for some time. The residual fug in her house would have kept her lungs satisfied for a week.

Nellie Gribben offered encouragement and hope to Bridget that World War II would soon be at an end and expressed her delight that her neighbour's son, John, was once more spending the night with his maternal grandparents to give her a deserved break. It had been a weekly ritual for a year, an arrangement that afforded his mother some much-needed respite. It also gave the boy a weekly change of scene and Bridget time to rest after her half-day Saturday morning six-hour shift at Cox's, a day and a half before her treadmill was once more activated. Monday mornings came around far too quickly.

On weekdays, when Bridget worked her 6am-6pm stints, John, like other children of his age in Tipperary, would 'see to himself' and make sure he was at school before nine o'clock, hungry from a lack of breakfast and hoping not to incur the wrath of Miss Sweeney and her leather belt, deployed with ferocity and a certain degree of pleasure on to the hands of boys – it was always the boys - who were late, impertinent or wrong with their sums. Corporal punishment was part of school life and many teachers saw it as a perk of the job.

St Mary's primary school sat conveniently adjacent to the Catholic Church of the same name – education and salvation side by side - although the proper title of the place of worship was the Church of the Immaculate Conception, too much of a mouthful for Lochee's Catholics. St Mary's would do. The close proximity of the buildings meant the entire school population would march the few yards between the front doors of the respective premises for Mass on every one of the many holidays of obligation in the Catholic calendar; each and every service bringing tedium to young boys and girls, especially if the Bishop was on the altar. When he put in an appearance, it would be High Mass and an extra thirty or forty minutes of hymns, prayers and kneeling on hard, unpadded boards in the front of each pew. There was also the extended sermon as eyes closed and heads drooped forward. All the while, eagle-eyed teachers would watch for misbehaving boys. Breaking wind, producing other similar noises and making remarks about their peers, sparked stifled giggling. It brought ferocious retribution in the form of a swift smack to the back of the head of whoever found the occasion linked in any way to humour.

Like his classmates, John's mind drifted from reading and writing lessons and avoiding Miss Sweeney's sore-hands sanctions, to thoughts of post-school football at Lochee Park where he was Jimmy Delaney, the Celtic winger, and the end of the game was signalled by the six o'clock bummer, a wail similar to an air-raid warning and heard all over Lochee. It sounded the close of the working day for the mill and was the starting gun for women to race for home where their kids, their house keys dangling from their necks on string, wondered what meagre meal would be served up for them by worn-out mums.

Nellie, in battered slippers and stained pinafore, wrapped across her body, warmed her hands on a mug of stewed tea and ruminated as she stared at the dying embers in the hearth of the tiny kitchen that also acted as a living room and bedroom. The high double bed was wedged into the recess below the sloping ceiling above which was the wooden staircase that led from the landing to the two garrets above.

'Any news of Frank?' Nellie dipped her curious toe into the water.

Bridget chuckled as she took her seat opposite. 'Are you kidding? News? From the great communicator? No, he doesn't write. Well, not since last Christmas. That's the last I heard from him.' She counted on her fingers. 'Five months. Can you believe it? Five months and not a bloody word.'

Nellie misplaced her diplomatic approach for a moment. She prodded a little more, perhaps hoping for a snippet of information she could dispense to fellow customers at Ugly Boab's corner shop the next morning.

Nellie fumbled for continuity in the conversation by underlining Bridget's earlier remarks. 'As you say, he was never a writer.' She paused for a moment, touching the hairs that sprouted from a mole on her chin as if she were checking they were still all present and correct. The response she wanted never came. She would not be thrown off course.

'Still, it's worrying' she continued. 'Your man away to war and not a word of how he is, where he is; if he's all right.'

Bridget's hackles rose ever so slightly. Her tolerance level beginning to be tested, she pursed her lips and inhaled through flared nostrils. This woman may be a neighbour and friend, she thought, but she was not inclined to entertain another of her interrogations. It had to be nipped in the bud. *She* was allowed to complain about Frank, but she would defend him to the hilt were he to come under fire from others.

'Nellie, we're at war,' she snapped back. 'Two bloody years of it. God only knows where he is. When he wrote at Christmas he didn't even say where he was. Or whether he was up to his neck in blood and snotters. I don't suppose writing home's a priority; not if you've got things like that on your mind.'

Nellie's stubborn streak would not permit her to be side-tracked. Not yet. She had just started. It was too soon for her queries to be quelled and her curiosity curtailed.

'Well, at least he could have acknowledged your letters.' She soldiered on with an air of righteousness. 'Could he not have sent you one of those printed postcards? You know, the ones the army has done for the men. They just score out what they don't need. You know ... I'm well ... I'm no' well.'

Bridget felt on the back foot, as if she had to present some form of mitigation for her irresponsible and unpredictable husband.

'Look Nellie,' she said abruptly in a tone that was a shade more hard-nosed than soft sell. 'Frank is Frank. He won't be bothered writing letters. You know how he is. He's always been one for the pals, the drinking, the laughs ... aye, and the patter. And we, me and John, are just a wee bit further down the pecking order.'

'Huh!' Nellie crossed her arms and gave a look of having been scolded, put in her place. 'He should never have got married, if you ask me. He's not the type.'

'Would you listen to yourself? Just because he hasn't dropped me a line doesn't mean it's the end of the world. We've all got to get on with life. Me and John. That's how I see it, anyway.'

A hurt expression like a child chastised, descended on Nellie's visage. She sought a path away from a potential clash as she considered her next line of questioning. She gulped her tea, took three loud swallows to get it across her throat and changed tack quickly. She doused the source of a possible quarrel and asked about John. Her query brought a smile to Bridget's tired but pretty, small-featured face.

'He's just fine,' she answered. 'Just like all nine-year-old boys. Thinks he's a man. Maybe he feels a responsibility, what with his dad being away. But he is bursting with excitement because he's getting a trial for the school team. Honestly, you'd think it was a cup final coming up. He demanded to know why the school strip was blue and not green and white like Celtic's. He actually asked the headmaster that. Can you believe it? The cheek of him.'

The earlier frostiness had thawed and the women laughed when Bridget reported that Mr McDonald, the St Mary's headmaster, had answered indignantly that 'we're St Mary's, John McGarrity, and blue is Our Lady's colour'.

Life in Tipperary was seldom dull, despite the hardship. It was a community full of characters and conmen, idiots and incidents, escapades and explosive occasions when anger and frustration, borne out of despair, depression and their fellow traveller, poverty, tipped people over the edge.

Yet, humour was always somewhere in the mix and gossip was a valuable currency, even if it was merely to repeat a story about a schoolboy's conversation with his 'heidie'.

3

Like most of Lochee's male community, Frank McGarrity had been a rank and file 'kettle-biler', the term used for unemployed men whose principal function in life, it seemed, was to boil a kettle of water on the gas hob in time for the return home of their wives after a 12-hour shift in the mill. That was their contribution to family life, to ensure the water for the tea that would be made in heavy teapots for the arrival of the woman of the house would be would be boiled. Then, the men would read the paper and watch the provider not only brew that tea, but conjure up an approximation of a meal for them and their children.

None of the men noticed that women of all ages were at the end of their tethers trying to cope with everyday life. Or if they did, it was never discussed. It was simply accepted and was not a topic working-class men deemed one for debate. It would only lead to outbursts and arguments, they thought; disputes where there was no winner.

If a woman could not cope and went into a state of depression, she was deemed to be suffering from 'nerves'. Mental illness, other than that which could be seen to affect a person physically, hadn't yet been 'invented' in working-class Britain.

The communal rut was deep enough to accommodate everybody. There was no way out of it, no light at the end of a tunnel that just became darker with each passing day. For many, there wasn't even a tunnel.

By 1900, Dundee had more than a hundred mills. The biggest was the Cox family's Camperdown Works, the largest in the world, covering thirty acres and employing 5,000 workers. It boasted its own railway, foundry and a network of little streets, the size of a rural village.

But, with the smell, smoke and smog came long hours and low wages. Less than twenty years earlier, much of the limited work for men in the mills was done by child labour as barefoot ragamuffins were sent out to earn and contribute to their households. Those in charge of Cox's and other mills turned a blind eye to this practice, at least until the under-aged workers were captured by the 'school board', men with notebooks who would trawl the various works and warehouses in search of truants. The boy employees would then be returned to the classroom with a stern warning. Until next time.

*

The kitchen sink at 13a and alongside it the wooden bunker into which the weekly delivery of coal was dumped, faced on to the rugged ground at the back of the building, reached by the steep stone stairs on which John frequently tripped and skinned his knees. There were metal hand rails at each side, useful to the men, and often women, who had imbibed too much on a Saturday night and needed to cling on to something to keep themselves upright.

Hot running water was a fantasy for the residents of Tipperary. The multi-purpose sink acted as a basin for washing crockery, cutlery, faces and armpits, the last two administered with a chunky bar of red carbolic soap, the scent of which was distinctive and overwhelming, like a sort of medical potion or, as some even thought, of leather. Still, it did the job of tackling germs and grime.

At some point over the weekend, usually a Friday night, the tin bath would be brought out, filled with hot water boiled in the kettle and in various-sized saucepans heated on the gas cooker and on the coal-fuelled hearth, and Bridget would bathe before John took his turn in the same water. On request, John would soak his mother's back and rub it with the deep-cleansing soap.

But John was not at home as Frank watched from beside an air-raid shelter and saw his wife draw makeshift drapes in order to comply with the blackout regulations requiring all windows and doors be covered at night with suitable material. Curtains, proper ones, were seen as a luxury, which meant that windows were sometimes blacked-out using cardboard for this nightly ritual. A glimmer of light that might aid enemy aircraft or possibly worse, spotted by civilian ARP wardens, could land the offender in court. Wardens, however, were seldom brave enough to wag fingers at Tipperary's women.

Frank's final steps as he slowly took the staircase to 13a produced a kind of anxiety in his stomach. How would Bridget react? It had been such a long time since they had set eyes on each other. Was her love for him still intact?

The tap, tap, tap on the door caught Bridget by surprise. *Nellie's left something. Maybe the People's Friend. She's forgotten to take it.* The 'have you finished reading it?' question occurred every week. Sometimes Nellie would pass on a Woman's Weekly, purloined from another acquaintance, as part of a swap deal. Bridget picked up the publication from a chair and took it to the door, never wondering that her neighbour had not waited for it to be answered. Usually, she would just walk in after a couple of warning knocks followed by an 'it's me' announcement.

But it was not Nellie. Instead, Frank, a forlorn sight, wet and worn-out, stood in the doorway and whispered: 'Hello Biddy.' It was the affectionate term used for many of Ireland's Bridgets.

Her mouth turned dry. She was stunned into silence by the apparition before her. She froze and stood like a statue and reminded herself that she hadn't heard from him for five months, hadn't seen him for two years, not since he headed off with many other Dundonians to their respective regiments. She could only stare for a few moments. 'Frank …What? … How did … ?' The words wouldn't come.

He stepped inside and the two embraced. He cupped her face in his hands and stared into her green eyes.

'Am I dreaming?' she said. 'Why didn't you get in touch? Tell me you were coming. God, what a surprise.'

Frank kept his voice low. He did not wish to waken his son, he explained, until Bridget informed him John was at her mother's for the weekend. He groaned as she helped him ease his way out of his damp heavy wool tunic and guided him to his old armchair with its stuffing creeping out of burst seams. Attentively, she knelt and removed his black hobnail boots, unveiling blood-stained socks sticking at the heels and along the tops of his feet where they met his toes.

He kissed her. He couldn't stop kissing her. But Bridget was full of questions: Why hadn't he written to alert her of his visit? How did he manage to wangle leave? Where had he travelled from?

'It was all a bit short notice.' Frank kept his explanation brief and to the point. 'They said I could have some leave. I wasn't going to argue.'

Yet, Bridget's welcome was surprisingly tepid. There was an awkwardness between them, partly generated by Frank's absence and his failure, perhaps unwillingness, to correspond. There was much going on in his wife's mind, though they were unconnected with the despondency of her struggles in negotiating each day and what it threw at her.

She managed to mask her deepest feelings and had no wish to pour cold water on neither the moment nor her husband's undoubted enthusiasm. She did her best to remain upbeat with a display, albeit it forced, of happiness. The least she could do, she thought, was show that the man seated before her was, despite his past indiscretions and false promises, still the one to whom she pledged love and obedience 'till death do us part'. Yet, while he may have been convinced, deep down she knew her performance was half-hearted.

They kissed; a long, lingering coming together of lips. The silent looks at each other's faces were penetrating, as if they were mesmerised at seeing something wonderful and spectacular for the first time. Despite this, Bridget could not dredge-up any feeling of love for her soldier husband. If Frank cottoned-on to her lukewarm response, he did not show it.

At last, she broke free from his arms. 'You'll be starving. Let me get you some tea. Heat you up a bit.'

Frank sat back in his chair. He sighed deeply. It told the story of relief that he had made it home. He confessed that he had thought on several occasions during the journey that surrendering to the travails he had faced over many arduous hours in the night, might have been a better idea rather than to scontinue.

'How long are you back for?' Bridget washed two mugs stained brown on the inside from years of thick, black tea, as the kettle boiled slowly on the ancient gas cooker. She dried excess water on her hands on the front of the pinafore she donned every day after work and patted down her hair.

'A couple of days,' he replied sheepishly, almost inaudibly.

Bridget's shock was palpable. 'A couple of days?' Her voice rose. 'Two days! Is that all?

'It's better than nothing, Biddy. I was desperate to get home to see you and John. I'd have done anything. I've been on the go for about eighteen hours.'

'Eighteen? You must've left at a queer time.' She busied herself at the bunker, her back to her husband.

Frank was momentarily hesitant, careful and deliberate in his choice of words. 'Aye. Well. About eighteen. Something like that. There was a delay with the travel warrants. Red tape, and all that. I just had to take what was on offer. And it's not easy to get from Swansea to Dundee.

'Swansea? So that's where you are?'

'Our camp's there, at least for the time being. Before they send us off somewhere else. When that'll be, I don't know. Just waiting for orders.' There was an eagerness in his voice to change the subject, to halt the questioning. 'Never mind me; what about you? How have you been?'

Bridget placed some bread, spread with dripping from the frying pan in which she'd cooked a rasher of bacon and an egg at tea-time, on to a plate and brought it to the small table that sat against the short part of the wall between the bed recess and the front door. Frank took his seat opposite the chair Bridget was about to occupy. Her grey pallor and expressionless eyes mirrored the grind and long hours of mill work that presented her daily with a sense of hopelessness. She portrayed an air of defeat, the most recent years of her slog of a life having drained her of faith and aspiration that the future would hoist her into a better life.

This, the poor housing conditions, the hunger and an inability to buy even the most basic of items for herself or, more importantly for John, was her lot.

15

'How have I been?' It was the debilitated sound of resignation. 'Where do I start? I work, whether it's the mill or the house, 'cause it doesn't clean itself. There's the rationing. And there's never any money.' She sipped her tea. 'Do you want me to go on?' There was more than a touch of sarcasm in her tone.

In a trice, the atmosphere was different, downbeat. Frank treaded warily. He leaned forward and took her hands in his. 'I know it's tough. But try to hang on, Biddy. The war'll soon be over and things will change, starting with all those mill owners. They're working people to a standstill and they'll pay dearly for treating us like slaves.'

But Bridget was in no mood to indulge him and listen to one of his political monologues, like those he would deliver to friends and fellow 'kettle-bilers' on street corners before he went off to war. The junction of Bank Street and High Street was the main venue for such gatherings - the Lochee parliament, some called it – and Frank saw himself as the local Lenin, a revolutionary, full of pipe dreams and promises.

She pulled her hands from his. 'Soon be over? Is that not what they said two years ago? It'll be done by Christmas, they said. Two wasted years and God knows how many deaths.'

Suddenly, she'd changed. She reminded Frank of the turbulence of their marriage and the numerous shouting matches they'd had. She had been unable to handle his womanising and drinking. At that moment he struggled to cope with her remarkable ability to switch moods.

Such rows had often been brought to a vicious and swift conclusion by the back of his hand on his wife's face. Memories of such a form of chastisement never faded.

But this should be a happy time, Bridget thought. She knew she needed to shake herself out of her present frame of mind, for his sake. She mustn't be selfish. He may be a waster, she thought, but he is fighting the Germans. She gazed at her husband and was thankful that, despite the horrors of war, he was still alive. 'Has it been bad?' She lowered her voice and drank from her mug.

Now, more relaxed, his body having heated up and the tea and bread tasting like a meal fit for a hero, Frank spoke of life in the Pioneer Corps. He confessed it wore him down. He was at rock bottom.

'All that shit-shovelling; fetching, carrying, digging trenches,' he said. 'We're just the ...' He shook his head and stuffed the last piece of thickly cut bread into his hungry mouth. ' ... labourers. The pit ponies. We clear mines, we guard bases, lay prefabricated track on beaches. Oh, and we fight, too.' He caught himself for a moment. 'At least there are some really decent men among us. Aye, and some hard nuts.'

It was a statement that brought a hint of a smile to Bridget's face as she remembered the physical clashes in which he had been involved over the years. Not that she'd witnessed any of them, apart being a competitor in their own private battles in which she inflicted at least a little damage before coming off worse.

'Well, hard nuts never bothered you.' She indulged him. 'Not when you've grown up around here.' Her brain then clunked into a gear of slight apprehension. 'Please tell me you haven't been in trouble. Is that why you're here?'

'No ... no trouble,' he insisted. 'Well, except for a couple of "moments" with one man. We call him the bloodsucker.'

'What is he, an officer or something?'

'That'll be right. He'd like to be. He's a sergeant. Acts like an officer. Three bloody stripes. Suddenly, he's Montgomery. Or Rommel, more like. He's halfway up the captain's arse trying to impress. Apart from him, everybody's okay. Well, most of them, and you know something, Biddy, I've learned a lot from them.'

This admission prompted her eyebrows to lift. Was this the same man who knew it all? Who would never accept that somebody else's point of view could be correct, even just a little bit? Could it be that, after almost ten years of marriage, with John coming along soon – too soon - after the wedding he had matured courtesy of being among comrades not ingrained in Lochee culture?

'The men; they speak about the love and respect they have for their wives and their families,' he revealed. 'They *speak* about it, Bridget. Not openly, mind. But if I'm chatting to them individually, you know, they're so optimistic. They look to

17

better times ahead, once the war's over. These blokes are just like me. They're political. And they're passionate about how the workers will call the tune when the fighting's done.'

Frank was now back where he liked to be, where he felt comfortable; on his high horse, spouting his views or regurgitating those of others whose opinions impressed him but who would never be given credit.

The cynicism in Bridget's voice was not exactly absent. 'Aye, and I suppose you'll be the one to march up to the bosses at Cox's and tell them what's what on behalf of the workers; in other words, the women. Because if it wasn't for us, there wouldn't be any jute coming out of that mill. God only knows where the jobs for the men are going to come from.'

But McGarrity would not be silenced. This was Frank the filibusterer, as if he was Keir Hardie addressing a group of trade unionists. 'You mark my words, Biddy. Change is coming. A better chance in life for everybody. Not just the haves in society, but the haven't got a pot to piss in lot, too. And, who knows, maybe I'll find work and we'll get out of living in a shit-hole like this.'

His filter had momentarily been switched off. She was not displeased that the focus of his speech had drifted from his 'our lives will improve' flannel, but his last remark stung this house-proud homemaker. He had crossed a line and recognised his folly the instant the words had left his lips.

'A shit-hole, is it?' Mrs McGarrity's disposition swung like a pendulum. Indignation rushed to the surface. 'Thanks very much. Is that what you think of my housekeeping? And by the way, I'm happy to hear you're going to break the habit of a lifetime and get a job.'

If Frank was good at anything, it was how to soft-soap someone and slither his way out of a corner. The people of Lochee knew that. Some considered him a likable rogue, the kind of person who shouldn't be taken too seriously. A chancer with hubris to match that of Macbeth. Others regarded him as a braggart and blatherskite with a giant-sized ego enveloped by arrogance and displayed with a twinkle in his eye that he believed disarmed everyone who entered his sphere. He could, however, at least on rare occasions, be charming, not to say diplomatic, especially when challenged by someone he knew would be too much of a handful for him, physically. His silver-tongued rhetoric had often been brought out for an airing when he admitted to himself that he might be on to a hiding.

But Bridget knew him better than himself. She was not of a mind to rein-in her anger. It didn't matter that his earlier 'shit-hole' observation was not designed to hurt. He was, he pointed out, theorising about Lochee, about Tipperary. It was a generalisation, he pleaded.

'My point is this,' he explained timidly. 'I know I haven't shown it before, but you need to know that I *do* appreciate you and what you do for me … and for John, of course.'

Would that be sufficient to mollify her?

No. Bridget would not be placated. The rage which had been bubbling inside her in the two years she had been left as a single parent, boiled over. 'Oh, cut out the blarney Frank McGarrity. Be honest with yourself. Look at the rut we're in, that everybody's in. We've been in it since the minute we arrived in this world. What have we got out of life? Think about it. And another thing; hand on heart, Frank, what have you contributed to this marriage? *Really* contributed.'

4

He was a man of strong character. His superiors thought so. They admired his largely understated, yet firm, style. He was able to extract the best from the men he oversaw and there was recognition in the officers' mess that, had he been from their class in society, he would most certainly have been among their ranks. Doubters, on the other hand, believed his Yorkshire accent might have been a hindrance in a world of public school voices.

Bert Leitch was held in high regard, too, by his peers, men of a similar background not unacquainted with life's harsher side. They respected him and admired his integrity, and when there was a task that required supreme responsibility and someone of authority to handle it, Leitch's name would invariably top the list.

'The man from the north,' was how the plummy-voiced, moustachioed men in the smart uniforms of a captain, a major or a colonel, described the well-read soldier, self-educated with a keen interest in politics and history. Those few in the lower ranks who did not warm to him because he was a stickler for rules and regulations, however, had a different label for him, one that was not complimentary.

'We have a little problem,' a weak-chinned lieutenant told him. 'We need you and another volunteer, one of your choosing, to take a little trip to Scotland to retrieve some lost property.'

All was explained and a deadline set, and Leitch didn't have to think twice over the choice of his travelling companion, a stripling of a lad, still suffering bereavement and having witnessed the kind of sights and experiences no youngster should have to encounter.

The order had been given, the plan laid out. Soon, the pair were on their way.

*

The temperature on one side of the small, stained, kitchen table had not subsided. Bridget was still fuming and Frank was grateful his son was not around to hear what had not been an uncommon occurrence over the decade since they tied the knot at the Church of the Immaculate Conception. She was just eighteen, he six years her senior.

Arguments, anger, strain and frustration in marriages were symptomatic of the time and the conditions, and the McGarrity partnership was not exempt, even now in what ought to have been a loving reunion following a lengthy period of estrangement.

Frank was eager to defuse the situation as swiftly as possible. 'I know I haven't contributed as much to our marriage as I should have, but I've just travelled hundreds of miles to see you and John. I thought you'd be pleased to see me.' He pushed his plate towards the middle of the table and stood up. 'I'm trying my best.'

Bridget knew she was behaving badly, but she could not contain herself. The lid was off the bubbling pot of exasperation, of being on her own, on the breadline, and doing what she could to prevent her son from becoming just another of the world's also-rans. Yet, she was not of a mind to soften her aggressive approach. As hot-headed at times as her husband could be, she was prepared to go for the jugular. 'Your best!? And what's that? Stopping drinking? No. Cutting down on your whoring? I don't think so.'

Frank's interjection was short and full of outrage. He was still on his feet, still struggling to understand why his wife was not thrilled to see him. 'Hey, wait a minute. That isn't fair. One wee fling and suddenly I'm Errol Flynn.'

'All right!' She stood up, too, as if it might add weight to her argument and jabbed a finger into his chest. 'Let's forget your wee indiscretion with that whore. You remember her, Frank? What was it they called her? Big Margaret. Aye, and I'll bet I know where she was big. She'd been with half the men in Lochee.'

Frank slumped back into his chair and shook his head. He prepared himself for the barrage that was coming his way.

'But let's put that aside.' Bridget went on. 'Before you went into the army, how much time did you spend being a father?

Now, you tell me we're going to see this new man, a caring man, after the war. Funnily enough, I don't believe it.'

Frank's exasperation was writ all over his face. In front of him was a woman possessed, one who spat out vitriol rather than being happy he was home and by her side. Was something wrong with her? Psychologically? Did she have 'nerves'? *She's gone mental. She's just given a bloody Olivia De Havilland performance.* Frank was not courageous enough, however, to express those thoughts out loud.

The heat had to be turned down. Of course, he appreciated her and knew the struggles she'd faced since he went off to war. He also realised that hearing his words about changing his ways, giving up life's shortcuts and becoming a family man, would sound foreign, laughable perhaps, to her. But he was, he stressed, being truthful.

History told Bridget that her wily spouse frequently spoke with forked tongue and could not be believed nor trusted. His next sermon, however, had her wavering.

'You see, these blokes in the regiment and me, we're all the same,' he said. 'The difference is that they're positive. They're already thinking ahead to when the war ends. They've got plans for the future. You talk to the people who live around here and there's nothing but negativity. It's all gloom and doom. Maybe it's a Scottish thing.'

With that, he moved to her side of the table, pulled her from her chair, held her tight and kissed her neck, her cheek and then her lips; a long, long kiss. Her taut body fell limp. Yet, he felt an iciness about her as he offered some words of comfort. 'Why are we arguing? I'm only trying to tell you how I feel. You'll see. Things *will* be different. I'll make it happen. You know I love you?'

Bridget couldn't think straight. *What did he just say? I love you? He's never said those three words before. Never. Not even during the rapid sex of ten years earlier that led to pregnancy and marriage.*

Frank welcomed the calm that swiftly descended on 13a Atholl Street. He believed that his reassuring words gave Bridget a glimmer of hope that her wayward husband was to become a new man. Maybe he *could* change. But did she care? Or was she merely too tired to carry on with the bickering?

For the moment, they could share each other's company, with Bridget accepting that she would be a sounding board for his hopes and desires, albeit a doubting one, one who'd heard it all before. At least for the time being, they could banish the cruel world outside and dream their separate dreams. There was also the not unimportant matter for him that centred-on his conjugal needs, but there was something in Bridget's manner and voice that told Frank her mind was elsewhere and that intercourse would not come easily.

5

He was persistent. 'Stay off work tomorrow, Biddy. Let's spend the morning in bed.' Frank was persuasive; Bridget pragmatic.

'That's half a day's wages,' she pointed out. 'And what do I tell the gaffer on Monday morning? That my man's come home unexpectedly and we made mad passionate love right through the night and I was too knackered for work?'

'Well, if you're going to say that, we might as well make it so you're not telling lies.'

As the ash in the fireplace lost its heat and the room became colder, he sat in the uncomfortable armchair and pulled her on to his knee and kissed her over and over again. His hands reached up inside her skirt. He stroked the bare skin of her thigh as if he were a teenager preparing for his first, fumbling manoeuvre en route to sexual intercourse. It was awkward, stilted, but his emotions would not be dampened. It had been two long years since he had been this close to a woman, the one he now held.

'No.' Bridget suddenly pulled back. 'Not like this. First, I'll wash the dishes and tidy up.'

Frank rolled his eyes in disbelief, but this was Bridget at her most practical. Thoughts of rising in the morning with dirty plates and cutlery in the sink were never entertained. And she could not depend on Frank tackling such a chore. Her mother had been a good teacher and she, in turn, had become a fastidious and organised manager of her home. She may be poor, but never unclean. Her domestic discipline throughout their marriage, however, had passed Frank by.

She kissed him on the forehead before grabbing a newspaper and thrusting it into his chest. 'And you can read this and discover that nothing much has changed. The women are still the workers and the men are at the top of Bank Street sorting out the world and trying to figure out how to establish the Peoples' Republic of Dundee.'

And, as if she was talking to an irritable child unable to amuse himself, she laughed and added: 'Wait you'll see, they'll want a Russian embassy in the city square with the Politburo honing their manifesto every Saturday night in the Pillars Bar.'

She indulged the various unsolicited points he made as he read the news while she tidied the room and brushed aside his notion that there would be a change of government after the war. The English, she insisted, would never vote out the Tories, especially if Hitler was brought to heel, after which she reckoned they would be ruling the roost for ever.

By now, Frank's ardour had been well and truly doused, at least temporarily. His attention was fully focused on the newspaper. He flicked through the pages of the Courier. Bridget was right, he thought, nothing much had changed. The stories centred principally on the war and anything and everything associated with it; battles won and lost, men killed or missing in action, rationing, the price of coal and numerous issues that affected everyday living. Page after page after page.

He was in optimistic mood and enthused about having a new house once hostilities were over, one with a bathroom and an inside lavatory. 'Lovely and warm, eh Biddy? Oooh!.' He closed his eyes as if to picture such bliss. 'Never again to be perched on a cold seat at the top of an outside stair with a force nine gale howling up your arse. Ahhh! Can you imagine what a perfect lavatorial experience that would be?'

Frank was now in a world of contentment far away from whatever happened in his everyday army life. The difficulties and discomfort of that long and gruelling journey from Swansea which brought with it all manner of osteopathic aches were now fading. At least, that's what his mind told him. He wanted to know about his son. He was also hungry for local gossip as well as tales of friends and acquaintances. He had a thirst, too, for scandal and bombarded Bridget with questions.

All she could think of was what it would be like in bed a few minutes hence, next to her husband's sweaty, malodorous body. It was an unappealing prospect. She found additional tasks to keep her occupied, as if she was playing for time to stave off the inevitable. She had been used to her own space for two years. *He's in the way.*

Frank reached the sports pages. He read about Celtic, his beloved football team, and a recent defeat to Partick Thistle in the Southern League. He made a few involuntary noises as his eyes scanned the columns of the broadsheet, its front page jam-packed with classified ads.

Suddenly, he sat forward in his beat-up old armchair and squinted in the light of the solitary bulb in the ceiling. 'Bloody hell!' The decibel increase shook Bridget, as if Frank had injured himself in some way. He was either shocked or excited. 'I don't believe it.' He startled his wife as she dried the crockery and stretched over the sink to double check that her curtain was tightly closed so that no shaft of light, however dim, would escape and attract unwanted attention from a jobs-worth warden, never mind a passing Luftwaffe Heinkel He 111.

'What? What is it?' she demanded to know, wondering if he had spotted the death notice of someone they knew, or perhaps a story of a tragedy or disaster involving people from Lochee.

'It, Biddy my girl, is only a very important piece of news.' He continued to stare at the newspaper almost in disbelief, re-reading the story that attracted him. 'Listen to this: Tomorrow, at Beechwood Park, Lochee Harp will play their arch rivals Dundee Violet in a crucial league match.' He placed the newspaper across his lap, put his hands together as in prayer and looked skywards. 'Thank you Lord.'

Bridget fell silent. Her eyes assumed the gaze of a serial killer; cold, detached, ready for dark deeds, a night of murder. She stood in front of him, hands on hips, a mix of disappointment and anger on her face. How could he allow a football match to interrupt his brief stay and valuable time with their son?

His soft-voiced, Uriah Heep-like plea - 'It's the Harp and the Violet, Biddy. You don't mind, do you?' – fell on deaf ears. He was concerned that her ire was just beginning to percolate. He accepted that not only did she occupy higher ground as he looked up from his seat, but that in every other way she had right on her side, and she knew it. Experience told him she could pack a mean verbal punch when required. He held his breath in anticipation.

She tossed back her hair and pointed at him. 'And what was all that tripe you were spouting a wee while ago? About being a changed man. Home for two days for the first time in a couple of years and what's top of your list of things to do? Watch a daft game of football.'

Frank, hoping to avoid a full blown bloodbath of a barracking, continued to test the water, to appeal to her sense of fairness. Every available man in Lochee would be at this football match, he pointed out. 'This isn't just any game of football, Biddy. It's special. Come on, you wouldn't want me to miss it. Would you?'

Her outrage ramped-up to fury on the temper dial. 'And what about John? When do you intend seeing your laddie?' This was the real issue for her. In truth, she would rather that he was out of the house, that he had not returned in the first place, although she would never dare say so.

McGarrity knew he had to box clever at this delicate stage of negotiations and think carefully and strategically over how to play his next card. After all, his wife was entitled to feel perplexed and utterly infuriated. He smelled further aggravation in the air. What would make his proposition acceptable? It was one that was simply resting on Bridget's permission not only to watch his beloved Harp against their most despised rivals, but to leave early enough for a pre-match get-together with pals and to reacquaint himself with Lochee's social scene. The plans and their timeline were already in his brain, but he was reticent to mention them at this point.

It was already in his mind that the venue for group fraternising would be the Nine Bells, the nearest and best of Lochee's public houses and where he was a regular before the Pioneer Corps came calling. But how to manoeuvre her towards sanctioning this; that was his next hurdle.

Bridget should have known that the undertaking about to be made would be hollow at best.

'I'll be sitting right here soon after five o'clock,' he pledged. 'Right after the game. Honest. I'll not let John down. I'd never do that.'

Bridget could not hide her despair, mainly on behalf of John. She slumped on to a chair, drained of energy, too exhausted to fight. The feistiness of a few minutes earlier had evaporated. Reality was in the room.

Frank now needed a meaningful gesture. He dropped to one knee in front of her, clasped her hands in his and told her not to fret. His mind may already have been on Beechwood Park, but he had to rediscover the magnetism that, in his mind, had won Bridget over when they first met. It was a charm, copied from the heroes of movies he'd seen - Clark Gable, in 'Gone with the Wind', or James Cagney, in 'The Irish in Us' - which had been instrumental in him bedding a series of women before and since Bridget had arrived on the scene. Would this current offensive work? Would another declaration of love, or something resembling it, pay dividends?

Bridget, too, thought of film stars when it came to Frank, but they were of the King Kong variety.

Her wry, disbelieving smile and slight shake of the head told him, wrongly, that she may have liked what she'd heard. That she believed wholeheartedly that he would, indeed, be with her and John soon after the final whistle had blown and talking his son through every kick of the football match. He should have known better.

'You just don't alter, do you?' Her tone was calm, flat, uncaring. He was suspicious and more than a little apprehensive. Where were the histrionics he thought were lurking somewhere? Was it a woman's trap, one into which he'd fallen from time to time over the course of their marriage? What was coming next?

She took a big intake of air through her nostrils. Then, with eyes that looked as if she'd been tranquillised, and in a voice as thin as old Canon Keenan's when dispensing penance at the end of a confession, she spoke not so much to him but to herself. It was as if she wanted to replay all the thoughts she'd had since she waved Frank off to war in 1939.

'Maybe we should discuss *me* for a wee while,' she said. 'Talk about *my* days, weeks, and the years since I last set eyes on you. Maybe we should talk about my half past five start to every day and how nothing ever changes for me. I sort out

John's clothes for school before I go to bed every night. I'm rushing like a mad woman to get to my work, to start my twelve-hour, back-breaking shift. But my mind's on John, hoping he'll be all right getting to school on time. I'm back at dinner-time to try and rustle-up something for us to eat, and then it's the same drill until the six o'clock bummer goes.'

Frank attempted to interject, despite most of her words flying over his head and his eyes indicating a lack of real interest in his wife's wellbeing. She held up an open hand.

'Just listen.' Bridget started to well up. 'I'm not finished. We can't forget the weekly wash at the steamie, hoping John'll mind to join the queue for my ticket. Sometimes he forgets, because he's playing football in the park with his pals and enjoying himself. Like wee laddies are supposed to. When that happens, I'm last in the line and John gets a battering. And I hate myself for hitting him.

'Then there's the rationing. Oh, and the butcher being closed on Mondays and Wednesdays. That's just in case I've got any money to buy meat, you understand. That's a laugh, eh? Beef; I can barely afford a pound of dripping and, if I'm frugal, a quarter of mince between us. And now they're talking about rationing clothes and shoes as well. Hollywood, it ain't. But do you want to know my biggest news, Frank? I'm sick to the back teeth of this life. If it wasn't for John ...' The tears trickled down her pale, tired cheeks. She wiped them away with a cloth she'd been using to dry dishes.

The signs were there for Frank; *approach with caution and choose your words carefully.* The venom may not have been fully extracted. He expressed his undying love for her. She meant more than anything or anybody to him. He repeated it, if only to draw a response. There was none. He stood and pulled her towards him. 'There are many things I admire about you, Biddy. Your beauty and your strength of character. There is nothing I'd change about you. You're everything a man could possibly hope for in a wife and mother of his child.'

With that, and in tandem, he led her towards the recessed bed. She could put it off no longer. Passion took hold, and emotions – Frank's – stirred. It was a night he had dreamed of in those traumatic, brain-pulverising times across the English

Channel a year earlier, although staying alive, he admitted to himself, had been a more important priority.

As they lay there, he told her of the dark days and horrible nights labouring in the Doullens area, near Amiens, where his group was threatened by the advancing Germans. He and his comrades reached Boulogne-Sur-Mer, but only after requisitioning a train following a fire fight with the leading German units.

It was survival of the fittest, or luckiest, he told her. The Germans and the Pioneer Corps engaged in fierce fighting at the barricades in Boulogne where the British soldiers destroyed a tank by igniting petrol underneath it. They were last to fall back from the perimeter with most evacuated from the harbour.

'I swear to God, Biddy, I thought that was it.' Frank spoke softly, as if reliving the horror of that encounter with the enemy. 'I could almost touch the bullets flying past my head. And Arthur …' His voice cracked and he took several seconds to gather himself before continuing ' … Arthur. Just a kid, Biddy. From Manchester. He was right next to me.' He had to pause once more. ' … The bullet went right through his left eye and took half his head away at the back as it … right through, it went. It was too awful for words. Others lay all around, howling, wailing. Bits of them on the ground.'

Bridget hugged him. She felt tears against the side of her face. She had never seen him like this. He held her tightly for some minutes. She kissed him, more in pity than anything else. It was a signal, he believed, that this hot-blooded soldier, desperate for intimacy, love, sex, had been given the green light to take things further and he was as lustful and lascivious as might be expected of any man in such circumstances.

It was obvious, too, from their first embrace that Frank could not engage in foreplay; too time-consuming. His passion could not be subdued. His love-making bordered on brutal, barbarous. Executed to serve a purpose unconnected with love. It was not Bridget's most enjoyable night on her lumpy mattress, but he was her husband, after all, one who needed the warmth of his wife's body.

6

They opened their eyes simultaneously and stared at each other for a few moments. She enjoyed the lie-in much more than the quick, unemotional, rough sex of the previous night followed by a serenade of snorting and snoring from her dead-to-the-world spouse. Mercifully, what could never be described as love-making, was all over in the time it took Bridget to run through an Our Father and two Hail Marys – she hadn't time to say a third, never mind a Glory Be to the Father - in her head. Frank's needs during the shortest of times of heavy, short breaths and prolific panting, as if he were in a 100-yard sprint, were satisfied and Bridget ran through an act of contrition, as she sought forgiveness. For what, she did not know.

That morning, all he could think of was that he was a soldier set loose and eager to make the most of his time back in familiar surroundings and to seek out those ready to update him on local current affairs, with a particular emphasis on affairs. Who was sleeping with who in Lochee and which of the criminal fraternity had still managed to escape incarceration?

Suitably rested, he was surprisingly spritely as he exited the bed and started shadow boxing, bobbing and weaving in his skanky underpants and vest, garments that had not been acquainted with soap, water and a washboard for some time. He made the familiar nasal sounds of a prize-fighter in action.

Bridget had already opened the curtains. She stood, one arm outstretched and the palm of her hand on the bunker, the other shovelling water from the tap into her mouth to wash away the taste of sleep, Frank's smelly breath and his sloppy kissing, as if she had come face to face with a happy, slobbering pooch reunited with its owner after being missing.

He continued with his left jabs and right crosses, uppercuts and hooks. In his mind he was Henry Armstrong successfully defending his world welterweight title against Barney Ross, just as he saw it on Pathe News in the Astoria in Logie Street a year before he went to war.

Bang, bang, bang! 'What do you think?' he asked as he threw a combination of punches. 'Still got it, eh?'

'Aye,' his wife replied, her back still to him. She wiped the excess water from her mouth before turning to remark that he looked lighter in weight and that his face was pale and drawn. She humoured him, though. 'Still, you're looking in the pink.'

It was a sop to his belief that he was a street fighter of note in Lochee and beyond. There were many, however, who took the view that Frank McGarrity talked a better fight than he fought. Few, if any, had actually witnessed him in action outside Johnny Dougan's boxing club, twice weekly in the evenings in the canteen of Cox's Camperdown works. But that was as a callow youth two decades and more earlier and into his mid-teens till booze and girls were given the nod over training and dedication. He was all too ready to brag of the threats and drunken proclamations on which he had delivered. Nobody could embellish tales of beating this opponent or that to a pulp at Maloney's Park better than Frank. They were largely fables with their origins in his own mind.

Edging a pasty-faced Bridget away from the sink, he splashed ice cold water from the tap on to his face then to his armpits before drying off. Bridget needed to sit down. She hoped she had sluiced away the remnants of the tiny piece of vomit she had projected unnoticed into the deep sink moments earlier, although Frank, wrapped–up in himself as usual, was unaware of it or even that she looked listless and devoid of energy. Rather, his mind was elsewhere, on Lochee worthies. 'What news of wee Frankie McGlinchey and all the others?'

'I haven't heard much of him lately.' She feigned interest. Her voice was low, her demeanour vapid. 'They'll be hatching their plots and schemes, as usual,' she said. 'They'll want to make sure we're prepared for a better Britain once the war's over.'

Her sarcasm went unnoticed. 'Well, they'd be right.' Frank said without taking his eyes off his favourite person as he looked in the mirror above the mantelpiece. 'Once we get rid of this government and the socialists are in power we'll be on our way.'

'You're away with the fairies,' she replied with the clear contempt she held for such talk. 'Fantasists; the lot of you.' Bridget could have kicked herself for opening the door to another of his orations.

Frank reminded her that his brother, Tommy, had moved into a recently-built Dundee Corporation house in nearby Beechwood, the area which was also home to the Harp. It was a housing scheme built four years earlier, when Germany was aiding General Francisco Franco's efforts to triumph in the Spanish Civil War and Hitler was already planning European domination, except Britain had failed to notice. If Tommy could be repatriated to Beechwood, why shouldn't Frank and Bridget find a way to unshackle themselves from the slums of Tip, as the locals called Tipperary, and be re-housed somewhere better? As he mused, he felt pleased that his brother had entered his calculating mind. He could be useful.

'John and me saw Tommy at Mass a couple of weeks ago,' Bridget said. 'He's looking well. Still working hard in the boatyard. Even so, I don't know how he and Bella manage the rent for that new house. Seven and six a week. Can you believe that? *Seven shillings and six pence a week; every week.*'

'Well, he doesn't drink for a start.' Frank was still preening himself in front of the mirror, or 'the glass' as he called it. 'And you know our Tommy. He's always been a grippy bastard.'

By now, McGarrity was beginning to feel something akin to claustrophobia. He was going through the motions, pretending he was interested in domesticity, household bills and the cost of living.

Instead, his thoughts drifted to the possibilities of what he hoped lay ahead that day; the pub and a reunion with pals topped his agenda. As he sat back down in his chair and Bridget found chores to do, he picked up the Courier and annoyed her by insisting on reading aloud.

Trying his best Alvar Lidell impersonation, which wouldn't have brought a call from the BBC to join the newsreader at Broadcasting House, he began his script: 'Listen to this, Biddy.

Sugar is to be withdrawn from catering establishments next month to economise and save shipping space.'

'Isn't that terrible?' he added sarcastically, ditching his effort to ape Lidell. 'How are all those toffs in their fur coats, nae knickers and stupid hats going manage their morning coffee at Keillers without their sugar? It's a disaster.'

He amused himself, picking out tales of court cases, trawling the death notices for any familiar names and even reading out advertisements that covered everything from cars to clothing to candlesticks, useful if you were short of a few pennies for the gas meter and could actually afford candles. A smile creased Bridget's face and Frank was enjoying the relaxation. But their world was about to change.

7

Three heavy, thunderous thumps almost removed the door from its hinges, startling the couple. The banging broke the moment and brought the conversation to an abrupt halt. They looked at each other as if to say: 'Who the hell is that?' It was too loud to be Nellie, and the rent man had already been the previous evening. Bridget opened the door to be confronted by a policeman who was out of Frank's line of vision.

'Mrs McGarrity.' Constable Gourlay and Bridget were known to each other. He had been a frequent visitor to 13a Atholl Street over the years thanks to Frank's not irregular clashes with the law, usually for drunk and disorderly behaviour. 'I'm wondering if your husband's here.'

'Are you now?' PC Gourlay had expected her confrontational, arms crossed, chin-in-the-air attitude. In Lochee the police were the enemy. 'Why would that be?'

'Well, he's gone missing and ...'

'I'm here.' Frank's interjection was brusque and unforeseen. It shook Bridget. 'Bring him in, woman.'

She drew her head back in bemusement and her eyebrows went north before being drawn closer together in a frown. 'What's going on?'

Frank was even more stunned when he saw that the constable was accompanied by two men, Sergeant Bert Leitch, the 'bloodsucker' himself, and Private Stephen Cosgrove, also from his Pioneer Corps unit. For the duration, however, they were there in another capacity – as regimental policemen.

'Well, now that we've tracked your man down,' Gourlay told his companions, 'I'll leave you to it.' He nodded in the direction of McGarrity. 'But I'd watch that one; he'll have you believing the moon's made of green cheese.'

As the policeman departed and Frank rose to his feet, Bridget's eyes bored into the side of his head like an imaginary drill while he stared at his visitors, hate coming from his eyes like lasers. He swallowed hard but did not remove his stare as he dropped the newspaper on to the floor beside his armchair.

Bridget was puzzled. What had Frank conveniently left out of their conversations? 'Are you going to tell me what's going on?' she demanded.

The seconds of silence that followed prompted Leitch to introduce himself and his side-kick to Bridget. Stephen could hardly disguise his boyish delight at having been offered what he saw as a holiday, something to take him away from the drudgery of army life, or simply seeing Frank, the man he hero-worshipped.

Like a Chameleon, Cosgrove's eyes darted almost independently of each other between Leitch and McGarrity as if seeking permission to engage with his pal, whose patter and ability to make him laugh he regarded as a tonic in troubled times. He and Frank shook hands.

'Well, well. It didn't take you bastards long,' Frank said to the young soldier, ignoring the man with three stripes and a regimental policeman armband on his left sleeve. 'You must have been right behind me.'

Cosgrove, a 22-year-old slip of a lad, lanky and scruffy and looking in need of a good feed, laughed nervously. 'Great. Isn't it?' he said in his London accent. 'Okay, I mean, not for you, but me; getting the chance to see Scotland.' The glee was pouring from every pore.

'Shut up, son!' Leitch barked at his Pioneer Corps crony. Frank harboured a hatred of the premium brand for the sergeant, not just because he was a figure of authority, but for his assertive approach to his job and what he saw as an over-zealous use of his status.

Bridget had already fetched two upright wooden chairs from the front room which was also John's bedroom and from where at night the youngster could hear the clandestine comings and goings of the people of Tipperary in the street below. Women like Dark Aggie McGhee, so-called because of her mane of jet black hair. She was seldom short of an excuse to display her talent for fisticuffs with all-comers, male or female. She did not differentiate after she'd had a few Friday night drinks in the snug of the Old Toll Bar next to the Rialto Cinema on the High Street.

Aggie would have visited a pub closer to home, had she not been banned from all of them because of her argumentative nature and penchant for a punch-up. Indeed, many of Tipperary's residents could hardly remember a time when Aggie did not sport a black eye or a fat lip, or both.

There was also old Mary Ann McCarthy, one of many Glaswegians domiciled in Tip. She was devoted to her dog, a sneezing, snarling, wheezing, waddling Pekinese called Wullie that nobody liked. You always knew she was around because she would stop every few yards, turn to wait for her ancient, matted-haired mutt to catch up and shout:'Whaur's ma hairy wean?'

The women of Tipperary, strong, resilient, tenacious and determined to navigate their way through life as best they could, were nonetheless annoying for John during their long periods of title-tattle at the end of the close as he tried to sleep.

'I suppose you'd better sit down.' Bridget, still baffled by the visitation and the reasons for it, signalled to the men to gather round the small kitchen table. 'Now then, who's going to enlighten me?'

All eyes turned to Frank, wondering what kind of spin he would manage to put on his story. But before he could utter a word, Leitch jumped in. 'Your husband, Mrs McGarrity, has deserted and …'

'Hold on, you bampot.' Frank leapt to his feet, his index finger just inches from the broken nose of the sergeant's chiselled face. 'You're overstating things more than a wee bit, are you not? AWOL is what I am. Absent. Without. Leave. Got it?'

Leitch, barrel-chested and burly, expressionless and unruffled at the prospect of a physical set-to, kept his cool. 'AWOL, is it? Aye, when we're not at war, lad, which we are, in case you hadn't noticed. So, deciding you needed a holiday at this time means you're a deserter and that's why we're here; to collect you and take you back for court martial.'

There was more than a little menace in the message. 'Deserter? Could that be true? Or was the sergeant over-egging the pudding to engender fear and alarm in his prisoner's psyche?

McGarrity dropped back into his chair like a sack of potatoes hitting the ground. He had to play for time as he contemplated his next move in a game of chess about to get underway. Leitch remained silent to allow for that process to take place. Cosgrove picked his nose, wiped the contents down the thigh of his uniform and sniffed.

Bridget broke the silence. 'I'll make us a nice cuppa tea. Isn't that what you English always say in a moment of crisis? A nice cuppa?' It brought a smile to the faces of the bedraggled soldiers, if not to Frank's.

8

Bridget was still desperate to get to the bottom of this mystery that was unfolding far too slowly for her liking. Suddenly, Frank's appearance out of the blue, coupled with his fondness for challenging rules and regulations, not forgetting that he had travelled through the night, all began to add up. To what, she did not know, but there was a fishy smell to all of this, she thought.

She had known her husband long enough to know just what PC Gourlay meant when he warned the soldiers to 'watch out' for her husband.

Frank and Gourlay, stationed at Lochee's South Road nick, had history. The man from Tipperary and the big, burly cop from Angus farming stock, had grappled verbally and physically on a few occasions before the Pioneer Corps removed the Tip troublemaker from Lochee. Gourlay called him 'a slippery customer'.

Bridget placed mugs of tea into the welcoming hands of the tired-looking soldiers and fixed her eyes on her husband. 'This *leave* business, then. It was just a pile o' shite, eh? Nothing but nonsense.'

Cosgrove laughed and Leitch drew him a look that said 'keep your mouth zipped and let's hear what excuse he dreams up'.

'I couldn't tell you. How could I?' Frank replied in hushed tones as he drew up a chair at the table. 'There was no point.'

'No point?' Bridget began to turn the conversation into a spectator sport for the two tourists in the room. 'You must have known these men could've arrived at any time. What did you think you were playing at, Frank? Was it just a game to you?'

It was the opening he wanted; the opportunity for an Oscar-winning performance. But would it work? Step forward Francis Anthony McGarrity, rabble-rouser, recalcitrant soldier and, as he hoped to prove, raconteur with all the patter of a snake oil salesman.

'Playing at?' he asked rhetorically. A game? Time in my own house with my wife?' It was a promising start. He had thought of every word before its delivery and paused in all the right places, 'A couple of days just trying to remember what it was like to have a normal life again. To see *you*. Aye, and the bairn. That, Bridget, is what I was playing at. Now, *you* tell me ... what was wrong with wanting that?'

Cosgrove sniffed a couple of times more as if he was trying to recognise a smell to which he was unaccustomed. He nodded agreement and looked at Bridget almost pleading with her to accept that Frank had made an acceptable point.

Leitch was impatient. 'Look,' he pronounced matter-of-factly, as if McGarrity's plea of mitigation had been wasted on him, 'we don't really have time for domestic squabbles. Just get yourself ready. We're leaving.'

It was the kind of curt command his hot-headed host could not allow to pass. He threw himself at Leitch, knocking over the crockery, some of it already chipped, en route to the sergeant's throat. He grabbed him by the lapels of his tunic and with their foreheads practically touching over the centre of the table, he threatened to 'break your fucking neck' before Cosgrove placed an arm and a shoulder between the warring soldiers. He begged Frank to release Leitch. Silence, then arbitration, of sorts, followed.

'Could we just calm down.' The youngest person in the room took control, albeit temporarily. 'Frank. Sarge,' he implored. 'We're never going to get anywhere if we fight and argue. Frank, the game's up. You know that.'

McGarrity bowed his head slightly and sat down as if defeated. But there was still a barrow-load of rage inside him. A smile came across Cosgrove's face. He was pleased with himself. He exhaled loudly and slowly through his nose followed once more by a couple more short sniffs. Leitch kept shtum. The mood was hushed, uneasy. A peace accord was not yet in the air. Enemies were on each side of the battered little table, a hand-me-down from Bridget's parents.

Leitch's eyes never left McGarrity. He knew the trip from Lochee to a cell at Dundee's main police station in Bell Street would have to be executed in an orderly way and without

40

drawing public attention to the exercise. Nor could he risk the possibility that their prisoner would break free. For the moment, though, dialogue was a necessity if Frank was to embark on the sales pitch that still swam around his brain. Choosing his moment would be crucial.

The silence that enveloped the room was broken. Frank blinked first. 'I'll bet there was a queue when they asked for volunteers to come and get me,' he joked.

'Well, I was actually selected by the sarge. Lucky me. A bit of chance for a jaunt,' a cheery Cosgrove admitted. He glanced at his superior for confirmation that it was okay to relay that information. 'And, anyway, I've never been further north than Dagenham.'

Frank looked to Leitch. The venom that was in his mind was evident when he spoke. 'What about you? You wouldn't have seen it as a chance for a break, would you? No. You'd have seen it as your duty. This'll be the highlight of your war.'

Leitch shook his head disapprovingly. 'Look, McGarrity, nothing personal, but ...'

'Huh! Here we go. Nothing personal. I'm only obeying orders. Don't give me that crap. You're here because you love it; the thought of being the hero, tracking down the absconder and returning him to camp.'

Cosgrove, boosted by his earlier success as conciliator-in-chief, stepped in. He saw no reason to further stoke the fire of fury and now, perhaps naively, regarded himself as the mature person in the room, a kind of special envoy sent to a far-flung land to bring about a peaceful conclusion to a tricky situation with one of the natives. He declared the conversation too negative and over-strained, especially if the arrest and journey south to London King's Cross and then on to Swansea was to pass without incident.

Leitch was still impassive, giving nothing away. It unnerved Frank.

Bridget, not wishing greater upset in her home, nor the prospect of Old Joe in the attic above banging his walking stick on the floor to record his disquiet over raised voices, agreed with Stephen. There was the prospect, too, that Nellie might overhear discussions that ought to remain top secret, particularly if she found the need to sweep the landing just outside the McGarrity's front door.

'Sometimes I wonder if you've got anything up top,' Bridget snapped at Frank. Her scowling, vexed expression ensured Frank knew precisely how she felt. She tapped her temple. 'I mean, did you really think you were going travel all the way up here for a weekend without them coming after you?' She turned her gaze towards the dour Leitch and tried to lighten the mood. 'You're a right sour puss, aren't you? Come on. Let's make the best of this.' She was the epitome of common sense, the Eleanor Roosevelt of Atholl Street.

Leitch did not respond, but he could read what was going on in the mind of Private McGarrity, exasperated in the extreme that his bold excursion was about to be cut short. He was right about Frank's irritation. It gnawed away at the runaway serviceman. But was his resentment more about his social plans for that afternoon having evaporated in an instant? Or was it that he didn't see a way to rescue the situation? True to form, he did not accept this was the end of the road on his adventure. 'What time is the train?' He delivered his query almost nonchalantly.

Leitch pursed his lips, looked away and refused to engage.

'Eight thirty-five.' Cosgrove blurted it out, his eyes again turning to his superior as if to ask: 'Was it okay that I told him that?'

It was information that set-off a bagatelle in Frank's brain. His thoughts, devious and otherwise, rattled around his mind. Duplicity and deceit were his stock in trade. He needed a strategy if the remainder of the day was to produce anything resembling fun. He placed his hands on top of his head and leaned back. 'Well, there's nothing the army can do to me when you take me back, 'cause I am finished; I've given up.'

The long pauses in the conversation continued to disconcert Frank. He waited for the sting he suspected Leitch was ready to inject into proceedings. Despite an earlier sign that the arrest and transfer to the city centre clink was a matter of urgency, the sergeant appeared pleased to be indoors, seated and resting for a while. At least, that was McGarrity's reading of Leitch's body language and he had a story in mind that could play-out to his benefit.

With their transport south so many hours away, why would there be a need to rush things? Let the battle of wits commence.

Cosgrove's continued inhaling proved a distraction and interrupted the tone and direction of the debate. Sniff, sniff, sniff.

'Fuck's sake,' Frank snapped. 'You've been sniffing like a demented mouse looking for a lump of cheese since you turned up. What is it?'

Cosgrove fumbled his way towards an explanation. Bridget smiled and leaned from her chair next to him and thrust her mop of thick hair into his embarrassed face.

'Is it that? Is that what you smell? She was light-hearted with her question, not wishing her young guest to feel over-perturbed. 'It's eau de jute. It's everywhere. My hair, my clothes. It's my job. I'm a weaver.'

Even Leitch laughed as Cosgrove blushed, then whimpered: 'Oh. Sorry, Mrs McGarrity. I didn't mean any offence.'

Ever the opportunist, Frank perked up. Time for a history of Lochee, he thought, and how women were the glue that held the Tipperary community together. It was a similar tale all over Dundee, he told them, home to a hundred mills and thousands of hungry families.

Whether they liked it or not, Leitch and Cosgrove were about to be on the receiving end of a lecture about the environment in which they currently sat. The sergeant seemed content to allow Frank to ramble. No need for haste. Departure time was still almost twelve hours away. Besides, he and Cosgrove needed a rest.

'Let me take you back five hundred years.' The lesson was underway. His unsuspecting students, ambushed and now captive, were about to have underlined what they already knew, that the man standing before them, his back to the cold, lifeless fireplace, was blessed with the gift of the gab. And playing for time.

'Not far from here, maybe a couple of miles to the west,' he held out his right arm to signpost the direction, 'there was a loch – Balgay Loch - a lake, as you'd call it, and that's where the weavers' cottages were. They were at the eye or, in Scots, the e'e of the loch, hence Lochee.

He furthered explained that the loch was drained in the 15th century although a burn – 'that's a stream to you Sassenachs' – ran through the land, and tenancies were offered to people along the route of the burn with the water they needed for weaving the flax.

His education at St Mary's might have been limited, but his keen interest in the historical narrative of his birthplace rendered him quite the expert on all things Lochee. Miss Sweeney had done a good job on that score. He pressed on, despite observing that Stephen's attention span had already expired and that yawns were being stifled. Leitch, on the other hand, did show an attentiveness to which McGarrity latched on.

He was on a roll. 'Then, about the year 1700 along comes a Dutchman and his family. He was a linen merchant and he says "I'll have a tenancy". That was the birth of what was to become the jute industry, long before there was even a Lochee. Later, cue the Cox dynasty and the building of an empire with its mill just up the road. The biggest jute mill anywhere in the world, thirty acres of land and buildings, a business propped-up by slave labour, like Bridget. And me when I was still at school.'

He spoke of the desperate Irish people looking for work. The potato famine had seen to that. They needed houses. So, there was a constant flow of people from across the Irish Sea, and their descendants walking - '*walking,*' he stressed - from places like Glasgow, just like his mother did as a toddler with his grandmother.

'A *hundred* miles,' he underlined dramatically, 'because they were poor and desperate and starving and in need of an income, any kind of income. And when they reached Invergowrie, coming in from Perth, they saw Cox's Stack in the distance; this great red brick factory chimney with nearly forty furnaces feeding into it and reaching over 280 feet into the sky. What a sight. Can you imagine it? It was their Statue of Liberty. Poor bastards. Their journey was nearly over, but all they'd done was swap one kind of poverty for another.'

Leitch was transfixed. Cosgrove wasn't. As Frank spoke, the dozy private picked away at some loose threads he discovered on his uniform while Bridget had already extricated herself from the table to potter about the sink area, but not before she injected a little balance into proceedings.

'Credit where it's due, Frank,' she said. 'The Cox's gave Lochee the public baths, and the library and reading rooms. And Lochee Park.'

Frank theatrically batted away this piece of information with the back of his hand. 'Ach! It's the least they could have done.'

The history lesson had captured Leitch's interest. He thought about his own roots in Bradford and how the Luftwaffe had destroyed his home town with bombing raids that started the previous August. The look of melancholy on his face indicated sadness. It was a side of this uncompromising Yorkshireman that neither Frank nor Cosgrove had seen.

His voice was faint, his mind elsewhere. 'Aye,' he said almost in a whisper, 'well, we've all 'ad it bad over the years; working people, I mean. And you're not so different from millions of others. Show me a place that wasn't bombed by the Nazis last year. My own town was hit. A hundred and twenty high explosive bombs fell on Bradford.'

'Yeah,' said a muted Stephen, almost as if he was participating in the conversation.

The atmosphere was now more sombre, bordering on funereal. Frank approached the table and pushed his tobacco tin across it and invited Leitch to roll a cigarette for himself. Soon, the three men were smoking and engaging in recollections of the combat they'd witnessed, chief among which was serving with the British Expeditionary Force in France just six months earlier. Then, there was Dunkirk.

9

She had slipped out unnoticed and headed to Lochee High Street where she hoped she wouldn't be spotted by her gaffer, the charmless Ned Henderson, a stern Presbyterian who couldn't quite come to terms with why his paymasters would employ Catholics or *'dirty Papes'* as he'd call them, unconcerned that it was the *'dirty Papes'* who were keeping many of Dundee's jute barons in business.

'Economics,' the mill owners would have told Ned. 'Cheap labour,' was what they meant.

The sun made an infrequent appearance as the weekday smog dissolved and the numerous industrial chimneys at Cox's and other mills dotted around the immediate area took a rest from belching out their fumes. Brightness graced Lochee on Saturday lunchtime, a time for the women to seek sustenance and scandal as they moved between Liptons and Masseys and other, less expensive, grocery shops in search of bargains. Even outside mill hours, the grind continued. There was no let-up for the stronger of the genders.

The local branch of the Dundee Eastern Co-operative Society, known as the Sosh - nobody seemed to know why – was the biggest attraction and it was there in their cavernous branch on South Road that Bridget could buy all she could afford, though not everything she needed, and build up a spend that would bring her a much-welcomed pay-out of the biannual dividend, known as the 'divi', a rewards scheme for loyal customers.

Bridget gazed longingly at the large wooden butcher's counter at one end of the bustling shop and wondered if there would be any cheap off-cuts available or a bone she could boil for stock to make soup with two or three carrots, some potatoes, chopped turnip and some cabbage. John loved her broth, but he drew the line at tripe, a favourite of Bridget's, principally because it was cheap. The mere thought of consuming the lining of a cow's stomach many women would boil with milk, gave John the boak. Give him some cheap broken biscuits his mum would take home in a poke, however, and he was the happiest boy in Tipperary.

'Where were you this morning?' Cathie Bannon's question from behind Bridget made her jump as she waited in the Sosh queue. 'Sleep-in, did you?'

Bridget was disinclined to enter into the detail of Frank's unscheduled visit, nor the unexpected arrival of two strangers. Had she not 'posted' her Sosh book and its shopping list into the wooden box on the main counter, thereby securing her place in a long line of women, she would have made an excuse and left. She looked ahead. There were still several women to be served before an assistant would take her book from the box and shout out her name to signal she should approach the counter on which sat huge slabs of butter and the wooden paddles that would pat them neatly into the required amount. There was a large chunk of cheese, too, on a marble surface with the wire at the ready to cut what was needed. Butter. Cheese. She could afford neither.

'Here.' Cathie, still in middle age but with short, tight, curly grey hair and circular nostrils, a combination that made her look at least ten years older, folded her arms across her ample breasts and drew herself closer. She looked in all directions to ensure there were no eavesdroppers. 'Did you hear about Lizzie Burke?'

'She hasn't been thieving again, has she?' Bridget felt obliged to participate, and, anyway, titbits of information helped soothe the tedium of queuing. 'The police are never away from her house.'

'It's better than that. Lizzie's lassie, Jessie, asked Isa McCartney's lassie to come round for her after school last Monday.'

'Don't talk to me about Isa McCartney.' Bridget's interruption irked Cathie, itching to relay the best piece of gossip she'd heard for months. But she was off at a tangent and there was no stopping her. 'That woman tried to jump the queue at the steamie last week. Walked straight in front of me, she did. As brazen as you like. So, I say: *"Hey madam, I'll have you know I've been waiting here for twenty minutes"*. 'And she says *"Oh keep your hair on."* Bold as brass. Called me a moaning bugger. Isa McCartney indeed. High and mighty, she called me. I could have said plenty about her. Couldn't keep her knickers on when her poor man, God rest his soul, was away getting himself gassed in the Great War.'

Cathie was impatient and unimpressed by Bridget's steamie story. She was just bursting to tell her tale. She gave a deep sigh. 'I'm trying to tell you about Lizzie Burke. So, Isa's lassie goes round for Jessie to play, thinking she'd be in because the school got out early. But Jessie hadn't got home from school yet and Isa's lassie, Sarah ...'

'Oh aye, that Sarah, She's got a tongue on her, that one. Just like her mother.' Bridget was off again.

There was now exasperation in the extreme in Cathie's expression and tone. She looked to see how far the queue had receded. Would she have time to finish her yarn before the shout, 'Mrs McGarrity, please' rang round the shop? 'So, as I was saying, Sarah barges her way into Lizzie Burke's house shouting for Jessie. But what does she see? Lizzie in bed. With ... A... Man.'

'A man? What man? Her man's away fighting the Germans.'

'Exactly!' Cathie paused for theatrical affect. Her lips disappeared into a thin, straight line, barely discernable beneath her broad nose and the merest hint of a moustache. 'But her man's brother isn't.'

Bridget took a few moments to process this newsflash. She drew her head back into her neck, screwed up her face and looked puzzled. Cathie felt a certain pleasure at being the conduit of intelligence of such importance, such significance.

'Wait a minute.' Bridget picked out the bullet points of the story, one by one. 'Lizzie Burke?'

'Aye,' Cathie confirmed with one nod of the head and an adjustment of her right breast.

'And her man's brother. In bed?'

Cathie's eyelids closed slowly in verification.

Bridget's flow did not skip a beat. She was both astounded and pleased that soon, all Tipperary would hear of Lizzie Burke's extra-marital shenanigans. 'And Paddy away doing battle in the Black Watch. Imagine that. Miss prim and proper.

That really takes the biscuit. And her at Mass and communion every Sunday.'

The short silence that followed allowed Bridget more time to absorb what she had just heard as Cathie smirked in a gloating, satisfied way. It was evidence of her pleasure.

'I can't believe it,' Bridget was up and running again. 'Paddy's brother? So, that's what his reserved occupation is ... sleeping with his sister-in-law? Jesus, Mary and Joseph. What's the world coming to? That would've been a right shock for young Sarah McCartney, seeing, you know ... *that.*

'You'd think so.' Cathie chipped-in, 'but she didn't bat an eyelid. She just ran down the stair shouting: *"Jessie Burke's ma's in bed wi' her uncle".*'

The women laughed at the thought of the little girl unwittingly spreading the news like some kind of child town crier around the immediate vicinity of the Burke boudoir.

'Wait till Monsignor Kearney hears about this,' Bridget gurgled. 'And Paddy. There'll be a line of people ready to tell him next time he's home on leave.'

'Number 53, Mrs McGarrity. ' A prim Sosh assistant, tightly packed into her stiff white pinafore, opened the book she had plucked from the box and before Bridget even reached the counter, her messages, as the locals called their groceries, were being assembled, ready for her to place them in her shopping bag. But, as she smiled to herself at Lizzie Burke's impending newsworthiness around Lochee with her secret story about to break, she suddenly rebuked herself because she, too, had classified information. Now, she was consumed by guilt and hypocrisy.

*

She meandered around the streets, her eyes darting here and there. It was vital she saw a very important person. Bridget also wondered what kind of carnage there might be back at 13a where there was the potential for flying fists and bloodied noses in her kitchen. But her thoughts were not totally focused on those she left in her home. Instead, she ruminated on what had happened more than a year earlier, on March 17, 1940, St Patrick's Day, and a meeting that was to change her life.

49

Harry Lewis was nearer in age to her. He was tall, muscular and athletic. His black hair flopped over his forehead at one side, making him look younger than his thirty years, and he possessed a smile and a warmth that could melt women's hearts. There was also an in-built honesty and integrity about him.

Harry was a teacher at Ancrum Road Primary School opposite Lochee Park where dozens of boys from the Victorian establishment and from St Mary's would gather to play football for hours on end when the lighter afternoons of springtime came along. They played, not school against school, but within their own groups and for every Archie Coats or Charlie McGillivray – two of Dundee FC's stars – among the Ancrum Road boy footballers, there were any number from the Catholic school believing they were Johnny Crum or Malky MacDonald, two celebrated Celtic footballers.. There was scant contact between the two sets of boys, but when there was, it was reasonably cordial. Until St Patrick's Day, when football gave way to fighting; Catholics versus Protestants.

Swathes of boys would march the half-mile or so from St Mary's to the park in search of 'Proddies' and singing Faith of Our Fathers and the Irish national anthem, the Soldier's Song as they went. It was part of a repertoire they'd heard their fathers and grandfathers belt out when they'd had a few drinks.

The boys never understood what was emanating from their mouths, but the coming together of a platoon of St Mary's pupils put fire in their bellies for an annual ritual underpinned by ignorance.

Soldiers are we whose lives are pledged to Ireland,
Our fathers fought before us,
And conquered 'neath the same old flag
That's proudly floating o'er us.

Except there was no tricolour of Ireland, just sticks and stones and anything else they could use to batter the Proddies.

The 1940 skirmish was not one John McGarrity would forget. He was a St Patrick's Day virgin soldier pressed into action by his peers and older boys, the St Mary's brigade commanders, striding forwards with a 'let's kick the fuck out of the Prods' arrogance. On this occasion, however, they did not expect to be victims of guerrilla warfare.

The Ancrum Road army lay in wait on the perimeter of the scene of battle in the foothills of Balgay Cemetery, the traditional burial place for Lochee's Catholics, the Tims, as they were referred to. Others kicked a ball around, aware that the St Mary's boys had one aim, to capture them individually, shout 'Catholic or Protestant?' in their faces and when enemy members responded with the inevitable 'Protestant', sticks, fists and feet would rain down on them.

This time, though, it was a smaller than usual group of boys from Ancrum Road that dribbled the ball and scored goals between jackets and pullovers that represented the goalposts. They were there not to display their skills, but as bait. They had been 'volunteered' by older boys to sacrifice themselves for the cause.

As their dirty-faced adversaries approached with aggravation in mind and exhilarated by being about to inflict damage on the enemy, the cavalry, strategically positioned in bushes and behind trees, charged like savages, armed to the teeth and thirsting for 'Fenian' blood. The ambush was underway.

The smaller recruits among the visiting soldiers - St Patrick's Day debutants - came off worse. Mercifully, the bloodbath had been on-going for just a few painful and punishing minutes before it was brought to a sudden halt.

A shout came from somewhere in the melee. 'It's Mr Lewis. He's heading this way.'

'Fuck's sake,' were the two most used words heard from the site of the skirmish in the immediate, fearful moments as news rippled across the battlefield that a teacher from Ancrum Road was en route at pace to the scene.

They ran in all directions, some in tears of agony from their wounds. There were those who pointed to no-one in particular and threatened that 'my big brother will get you, you bastard'. One or two limped away in retreat, while others left the front line with a turn of speed that would have been the envy of Jesse Owens. Others displayed distress at the thought of their mothers assaulting them when they arrived home with bumps, bruises, ripped jumpers and skinned knees.

The Ancrum Road stragglers were sent on their way with a stern warning from Mr Lewis, a popular teacher, judged by his pupils as firm but fair. His words 'report to the headmaster at nine o'clock tomorrow morning' rang in their ears as they left the field of battle. There was the added worry that their mothers – it was always the mothers - might be summoned to the school to be told of their felony. It prompted a plethora of 'my mum will kill me' cries from those in retreat. This was a dark day for the freedom fighters of both religious persuasions.

As the park cleared, alone on the ground lay one casualty, unable to hoist himself up. He was devoid of the energy required to flee from authority.

Harry Lewis could see blood seeping from the crown of John McGarrity's head and across his black hair, but a closer inspection convinced him the cut was not deep enough to merit a visit to the casualty department of Dundee Royal Infirmary. Instead, after dusting the grass off the war-torn combatant, who revealed he'd been clubbed on the head with a piece of wood from a fence, Lewis took matters into his own hands.

*

Bridget's thoughts moved from Cathie Bannon's bulletin to that March day more than a year earlier. She was puzzled as she strode closer to the stairs that led up to her house. *Who the hell is that sitting on the steps with John?* Her second thought might have centred-on how handsome the stranger was.

'Mrs McGarrity,' said the man in the smart, grey suit as he stood up on her approach. 'I'm Mr Lewis, Harry Lewis, from Ancrum Road School.'

Bridget was bewildered. Her son, outside their home with a man from a school he did not attend. Her heart pounded. 'Has something happened?' She turned to John. 'Are you all right? Has there been an accident?'

As the events of earlier were explained, Bridget patted down her clothing and pushed her hair out of her eyes, trying to look tidy and presentable as the young teacher spoke. John sat on the stone steps with a look of contrition across his face before moving inside, deflated, ashamed and rubbing a sore head that showed it wasn't just his pride that was bruised.

There were many things that impressed Bridget about Harry Lewis, among them that he did not create a fuss over the Lochee Park showdown. It was the way boys behaved at that age, he said, and not the first St Patrick's Day confrontation he had broken up. What was the point in allowing bloodshed to occur because of ignorance, he insisted. Perhaps he understood that, as Bridget was on her own, without a man by her side – John had informed the teacher under interrogation that his father was 'away beating the Germans' – she didn't need additional worries. He played-down the re-enactment of the Battle of the Boyne. He had walked John home not because of his involvement, although he had given him a stern, teacher-like lecture on the negativity of sectarianism, but because of his injury. He also wanted to be sure the boy was safe from a potential Protestant bushwhack as he made his way to the security of Tipperary.

As they chatted, John waited in the house, anxious, apprehensive and concerned, not just that his mother's anger would result in him receiving some form of corporal punishment as soon as her discussion with Mr Lewis ended, but that he would have to confess his 'sin' along with the others he would trot out to either Father Butler or the fiery Monsignor Aloysius Kearney, a confessor to be avoided whenever possible because of a booming voice that echoed through the church.

It was not unheard of for this flamboyant Irish priest, who strutted around Lochee in a black cape, black beret and carrying a gold-topped walking cane, to make highly audible jibes to a sinner which could be picked-up by those in the pews as they waited their turn to enter his scary world, the dark confessional box.

'You did *what?*' Heads would turn and tongues would wag when Kearney made one of his many pronouncements of outrage and astonishment, and all eyes would be on the poor reprobate exiting the not-so-secret wooden structure as he or she tried to slink into the nearest seat to kneel and embark on whatever series of prayers had been ordered as penance.

So, avoid Kearney at all costs, thought John. Then again, the man from Kilkenny might be sympathetic to a boy who had put his neck on the line for Ireland, if only for a few misguided minutes. He ran through the script in his head:

'Bless me Father for I have sinned. It's been a week since my last confession.'

'Yes, my son. Continue.'

'Father, I was cheeky to my mum when she got on to me for not washing behind my ears.

'I had improper thoughts after Matthew Cassidy drew a naughty picture on my school jotter. And I swore when we lost a game of football in the playground.'

'All right, my son. Is there anything else?'

'Ye – yes Father. I was with a lot of other laddies who fought boys from Ancrum Road in Lochee Park on St Patrick's Day.'

'How many boys went from St Mary's?'

'About twenty, Father.'

'And did you win?'

'I think it was a draw, Father. I had a cut on the top of my head.'

'Hm! Fenian blood spilled, eh? The little blighters would have liked that. Well, my son, violence in itself is not a good thing, but on this occasion God will forgive you because your heart was in the right place. I'm not condoning fighting, mind. But if you're going to tackle the Protestants on St Patrick's Day, make sure you win. Now boy, off you go and say three Our Fathers and three Hail Marys and a Glory Be to the Father.'

John peered from the window and sensed the conversation his mother was having with Mr Lewis was drawing to a close. He also noted a rarely-seen smile on her face and a girlishness about her mannerisms. It was as if the cares she carried daily had vanished.

Bridget liked much about this handsome man; his courteous manner, his gentle voice, the softness of the hand that shook hers as he thanked her. For what, she did not know. He appeared keen to extend their conversation and felt himself introducing topics that were divorced from the issue he was there to address. But he did not wish her to believe it overbold and a trifle presumptuous to linger. After all, she was a married woman.

He was also aware that behind Tipperary's twitching net curtains there were the prying eyes of women already making up their own scenarios about what they were watching.

Bridget knew that, too. But a pleasant squirming sensation in her gut, one she'd never before experienced, not with Frank, not with any man, was sending messages to her brain.

What is this I'm feeling? I didn't know men could be so nice, so good to be around.

Harry felt a glow, a sensitivity from Bridget. He was impressed by her strength of character and her stoicism as he thought of the burden she carried, one of hard work and hardship, without a man by her side to share the load. He felt an immediate attraction not only to her pretty looks and beguiling smile, but to her warm personality and friendliness.

'It was good to meet you, Mrs McGarrity.' With those few words he walked off.

Bridget felt a flutter in her heart, like a giddy schoolgirl finding love for the first time. *Will I see him again? Don't be silly, Bridget.*

*

A packet of tea, some loose vegetables, potted hough, that 'some like it, others hate it', indigenous dish of stringy meat encased in gelatine which was a staple diet for many Dundonians, were in Bridget's string shopping bag as she left the Sosh to head for Lochee High Street. John hated hough, but it was cheap and nutritious and palatable for him when served with lots of mashed tatties to disguise the taste and texture. There was also his treat, the broken biscuits, a halfpenny giveaway because they were spoiled and fit only, as far as shop owners were concerned, for throwing in the bin.

But Bridget was on a more important mission that dominated her mind that Saturday morning when she slipped away from Frank and his two unwanted guests, too preoccupied with sorting out the world.

In the thirteen months since she'd first laid eyes on Harry Lewis, love had blossomed and her feeling of hypocrisy over Lizzie Burke's dalliance with her brother-in-law had been jettisoned from her memory. She moved up Bank Street and on to the main thoroughfare that, in one direction, took buses towards country villages like Alyth and Newtyle and to the berry fields of Blairgowrie, a popular destination for Dundonians when the jute mills were locked over the holiday fortnight. There, in tents and huts that were rented out, they could still have an income, this time from farmers needing pickers of their acres of raspberry crops.

Where the hell is he?

She recalled how he had confessed his visit to her home a couple of weeks after he had safely delivered John in the wake of the St Patrick's Day dogfight, had been a ruse simply to see her, that 'I wanted to check that your boy is all right' was not the prime reason for his return to Tipperary.

From that day, the couple would conveniently 'bump into each other' on Lochee High Street around lunchtimes on Saturdays. Each time, they would chat for a few minutes, smiling, sometimes laughing, before remembering a married woman appearing so happy in the company of a good-looking bachelor sent out all the wrong signals to would-be gossips.

It was on one of those occasions that the first invitation to visit 13a for his 'tea' one Saturday evening when John would be with his grandparents was nervously extended and keenly accepted by Harry. The excitement was instant and unmistakeable.

There's that strange feeling in my stomach again.

Within a very short time it became clear Bridget and Harry were besotted with each other. But both were aware of the issues this would bring, especially when the Saturday nights turned into Sunday mornings and leaving became a furtive manoeuvre for Harry, like a burglar departing the scene of his crime. They decided they would confront such problems when, rather than if, they arose. They were deeply in love and it was painful when they had to separate and accept it would be a whole week – seven long days - before they could be together again. Yet, they could not escape the reality that, in time, the toughest of choices would have to be made.

Where is he?

That Saturday, as she left Frank, Leitch and Cosgrove, she sweated over how it was vital she see Harry to warn him that their usual Saturday arrangement and another night of a thousand kisses, could not take place.

10

There was a cheery and unexpected ambience swaddling the three men in uniform crouched around the kitchen table. It was achieved largely by their cordiality and concentration on the card game of pontoon with each desperate to finish with most of the matches from Frank's box of Swan Vestas, the only currency available to gamble. Peace had broken out. The air was thick with smoke from the many roll-up fags that had been puffed with their fumes dancing across the faces of the card-sharps and, in light of the absence of hostility, the host seized his opportunity to push through a proposal that had occupied his thoughts since their arrival. But when to introduce it into the conversation.

He drew the last of the nicotine from a tiny dowpie before stubbing it out on the saucer that doubled as an ashtray. 'So, are you lads football fans?'

'I went to see the Arsenal once or twice,' said Cosgrove, as he sucked on the remnants of his cigarette, held between the ends of a thumb and forefinger. He looked at his cards. He found it difficult to disguise a smile. 'Didn't like it. Pretty boring, if you ask me.'

But McGarrity's narrative wasn't aimed at the youngster. He knew the private would go along with anything that would enhance this little diversion in his military life.

Leitch's ears pricked up. 'Boring? Never. You can't beat a couple o' pints and a game at Valley Parade. Derby games. Bradford City versus Leeds United or Huddersfield. Twenty-five thousand supporters. Well, that was before the war. A good bit before the war. We're in Division 3 now. Anyway, they were great days. I used to watch Arthur Rigby. Winger, he was. Played for England.' It was nostalgia time now for the sergeant as he looked at McGarrity and pointedly added that Rigby was in the England team that beat Scotland 2-1 in 1927. 'And George Murphy. He could play anywhere, from full-back to centre-forward. Welsh, he was. There was one time … '

'Aye, okay sarge,' Frank interjected. 'We don't want a history of Bradford City.' Leitch offered a wry smile, shook his head and took the insult on the chin. But at least Frank had established that the man across the table had an interest in the national sport and that was important as he navigated his way towards phase two of his plan.

'So, you like a drink and you have a love of football,' he confirmed. He glanced at the clock on the wooden mantelpiece with its lonesome chipped-eared wally dug, those ornamental china dogs most houses had. 'You see, I was just thinking, what with us having our own derby game today and the pub only a few minutes away, that ...'

'Hah! Not on your life.' Leitch threw his cards on to the table, face down. 'You're a chancer, McGarrity.'

Frank wouldn't be diverted. He knew Cosgrove's vote was in the bag, despite his earlier assertion that watching twenty-two men chasing a ball about a patch of grass didn't hold much appeal for him.

'Give me a minute. Let me finish,' he demanded. The Scot was measured and composed. 'Think of it. We've got about eight or nine hours to kill until the train leaves. We can nip along to the Nine Bells, couple of pints, and up to Beechwood Park for the Harp and the Violet. What a send-off that would be; us getting it right up those orange bastards. Back here by the back of five o'clock to see my boy, because Bridget's going to fetch him from his gran's, and then we'll be off. What could be simpler?'

Cosgrove pulled his cards close to his chest, impatient for the resumption of the gambling. After all, he was sitting on an ace of clubs and a queen of diamonds and had eight matches riding on his hand.

Leitch shook his head incredulously at Frank's submission. He reverted to his official position that, while he appreciated the Tipperary hospitality and how the earlier prospect of fisticuffs between the two had been averted, McGarrity had to accept he was a prisoner under arrest at the height of a war. That wasn't going to change, nor was the manner in which he and Cosgrove would execute their duty. They had a responsibility to return their man to camp. McGarrity ought to be in a cell at Dundee Police's Bell Street headquarters, he underlined, but he had been willing to slacken the rules, for Bridget's sake. It had been a tough resolution for him to reach, but that's why he was a sergeant, to make such decisions.

His little speech was aimed at Stephen as much as it was at Lochee's self-appointed favourite son. Cosgrove's inexperience, Leitch felt, could become a hindrance, especially as he worshiped the ground on which McGarrity walked.

'Pontoon!' Stephen blurted out excitedly when he spotted a gap in the discussion over what might or might not happen later. 'I've got pontoon.' He laid out his two cards for all to see. 'Ace of clubs, queen of diamonds.'

Leitch drew him a distracted look, and turned over his own hand; ace of diamonds, king of hearts. 'Me too; and I win, 'cause I'm the banker.'

'Fuck!' Cosgrove could not camouflage his consternation. The older soldiers laughed at his misfortune.

Frank, meanwhile, was not ready to leave the path on which he had embarked. *In for a penny,* was how he viewed his next move. If Stephen would back him, then maybe Leitch would, if not break, then bend; just a little. After all, there was no escape plan. Where would he go? He knew thoughts of the social gathering he outlined earlier – boozing in the Nine Bells - would still be buzzing around inside the subconscious of his house guests, considerations that would not yet have been erased. He was positive that, if they - well Leitch, because *his* decision was all that mattered - had a modicum of weakness for temptation, it would be found.

The peace that followed as the Yorkshireman gathered the cards, shuffled them and dealt another hand, brought a certain serenity with it. *Let's try another route,* Frank thought. Meanwhile, no-one seemed to notice that Bridget wasn't around.

*

The High Street was its usual bustling hub on a Saturday. Women busied themselves as they swooped on the grocers' shops or tried to keep their noisy children in order. For the district's inhabitants, young and old, the weekend had started in earnest. Mischievous, misbehaving boys, their parents at home or in the pub, roamed in small gangs of four and five to reconnoitre various sweet shops in order to determine what items of confectionary might be easily purloined.

Mary Peebles's establishment, packed with bonbons, mint imperials, wine gums and dolly mixtures, was always an easy target. The old dear would be asked for a quarter of sweets from a jar on the top shelf. By the time she had climbed her creaky wooden steps then descended with a heavy glass container from which she expected to empty delicious delights into the scales that sat on the counter, her young 'customers' were long gone. Their pockets were stuffed with whatever candy bars or other sweeties lay closer to ground level. Old Mary fell for this scam every time and barely noticed the cost to her of every heist that had lightened her stock of aniseed balls, liquorice sticks and granny sookers.

The urchins, with unwashed faces and holes in their pullovers, entertained themselves by pulling the hair of well-scrubbed, patient little girls waiting while their mothers exchanged hearsay outside shops. The boys, all known pupils of St Mary's, enjoyed taunting and teasing Tam the Pusher, a strange, short man in a stained raincoat and a flat cap, known for shoving out of the way anyone and everyone who blocked his path on the pavement, muttering abuse as he went by. The youngsters would shout 'plum nose' at him, a barb underscoring the colour of his snout that suggested Tam, not a social animal by any means, preferred his own company and drank whatever alcohol he could lay his hands on within the confines of his home in nearby Whorterbank. It was another slum enclave of jute workers and large numbers of Catholics, also on the payroll at Cox's, a stone's throw from that particular ghetto. There, in that other little slice of Ireland, there could be found O'Donnells and O'Neills, Dohertys and Doyles, all trying to scratch out an existence.

Bridget, her anxiety levels rising, walked up one side of the High Street and down the other. It was imperative she see Harry. The search brought exponential worry. She had to talk to him, to warn him. The potential horror of him arriving at her home that evening to find Frank and his Pioneer Corps pals sitting at the table was unthinkable.

Where in God's name are you?

She knew Harry would be somewhere on or around Lochee's main street looking for her. He was always there at lunchtime on Saturdays, hoping to see her and pretend it was a simple coincidence that they'd bumped into each other. It was, of course, designed to confirm their arrangements for their later assignation.

Bridget's runaway heart rate was brought under control when she spotted him leaving Alexander Alexander, the barber's shop known locally as Double Ecky's. It was where many Lochee men went for their short back and sides every few weeks and Harry looked as striking as could be as he stood on the pavement and brushed hairs off his suit with the palms of his hands.

A skinny man on a bike struggled to keep it upright. Its front wheel had caught in a tram rail and Harry shouted 'steady Rab' as the weedy creature, the bottom of his trousers tied with string to prevent them being caught in the chain of the contraption, fell to the ground.

'Bastard!' Rab snarled as he toppled and his rickety old Raleigh fell on to him before he continued to curse his mode of transport as he untangled himself and regained his composure while youngsters giggled and shouted jibes in his direction.

Bridget's heart soared when she heard Harry's voice. She crossed the cobbled street towards him, avoiding the tram bound for Dundee and its terminus in Lindsay Street, right next to the Old Steeple, the medieval tower with 232 steps that had withstood the ravages of time and invading armies for more than 500 years.

People would say to each other: 'We must go up the Old Steeple sometime and see if we can climb its stairs without having a stroke.' Few actually followed through on that thought, stuck in the recesses of minds from schooldays. 'Aye, that'll be right,' was the usual response when it came up for discussion.

Who knew that the lock on the door leading from the entrance hall to the 165 feet high tower's staircase was the same one that prevented Oliver Cromwell's soldiers from entering in 1651? Who cared?

Who knew that Cromwell's mob set fire to a heap of wet straw piled on the floor in an attempt to smoke out the defenders of the town, entrenched on the upper floors? Who cared? Certainly not the boys and girls of St Mary's, Lochee, although had Tipperary's younger ne'er do wells known there was still evidence the tower was once used as a jail and that the entrance hall still displayed stocks and weapons of torture like knee-grinding screws, their interest in the gruesome side of life and death might well have been tweaked.

It was right outside the Old Steeple that the Lochee tram stopped and locals who needed to 'go down the town', as Dundee was referred to, would disembark. That's all that mattered to them, not the history of this magnificent structure or the lives lost in its defence. Just that it was the final stop for the number 3 tram.

Like two spies lurking in the shadows – in this case at a close next to Double Ecky's shop - Bridget and Harry each played their roles as per the agreed Saturday script in case nosey passers-by suspected anything untoward was going on. It meant their time was brief. Harry's heart sank on hearing Frank was home, but he was less concerned that the prodigal was now in the company of two regimental policemen ready to remove him. The main thing on his mind was that it would be seven long days before they would next see each other, an unbearable thought for both. Still, better that than the prospect of the love affair being exposed and what might happen in the aftermath of such a revelation were Harry to turn-up to find Frank on his battered armchair.

How the couple desperately wanted to touch hands, to remain silent and gaze at each other for a few precious moments; to kiss. Too soon, their petit liaison was over. 'I love you,' she whispered, the tips of her fingers furtively touching the hand at his side before they turned to go their separate ways. They did not look round, but each felt overwhelmed with adoration for one another, their pulses speeding as if they were about to go into shock with sheer excitement.

*

The banter was highly audible. She could hear them – friendly, boisterous - and their laughs as she climbed the stairs towards 13a.

Nellie Gribben would also have heard the din. So would others in the block. Even old Joe in the garret, despite his deafness, a souvenir from World War I shelling at Passchendaele, would have been able to count the number of voices, probably with his ear to the floor.

Joe never spoke of his time in France, but everyone accepted it was likely that the irritability he displayed and the headaches he sometimes complained of, as well as his hearing loss, were the result of being subjected to the unimaginable battering his ears took as the Allies threw five million tons at enemy positions.

Unlike 80,000 other British soldiers, Joe did not suffer from shell-shock, although around Tip people said he had 'nerves', a condition many under pressure women, beaten by deprivation, experienced. Depression, it seemed, or at least a word to describe it, had not yet reached Tipperary.

Bridget had been in the house for a few moments before the military trio even became aware of her return. It was only when she interrupted the card-sharps to announce that she'd make spam sandwiches and fresh tea, that their attention was re-routed.

Frank, though, was still on a mission. He would not be swayed from his ultimate goal by the glee on the faces of Leitch and Cosgrove at the offer of something to eat.

'So, what about trust?' he asked, apropos of nothing in particular and breaking the concentration of the hungry RPs. His question was aimed at Leitch. 'Does trust come into your list of whatever it is you need to make decisions about as a sergeant? Is it tough to be trusting?'

Leitch's body language indicated a muted interest in continuing the debate and was McGarrity's green light for further progress to be made.

He invited Frank to elucidate. All the while, Cosgrove's only thoughts were fixed on trying to produce a winning hand for the first time. Luck wasn't on his side that day.

'What I mean is ...' Frank paused to find the right words. 'Would it be too hard for *you* to trust *me*?' Leitch looked thoughtful. Or maybe just befuddled. Private McGarrity's perseverance could not be questioned. 'Look, we're hundreds of miles from authority – real authority, I mean - and hours and hours to kill before we can make it back to that authority. So, if you're prepared to trust *me*, I'll make sure you have a day to remember; a day out in Lochee you'll never forget.'

He could see a glint in Stephen's eye. This was a tantalising dream for the youngster. Mind games were now at play and when the London lad became more deeply absorbed by Frank's overture, a window of opportunity was pushed open.

'The Harp are what you lot would call a non-league team,' Frank explained. 'We call them juniors, and the teams in action today are the Celtic and Rangers of the juniors. They hate each other. Their supporters hate each other. The supporters' wives hate each other. Their bairns hate each other. You'd love it.'

Leitch was relaxed. There was a grin on his face as he turned to his underling and chuckled. 'Don't listen to this shit. He's a bloody conman.' But the way he said those words hinted that he was warming a little to the laird of Atholl Street.

Frank ignored the remark and focused his attention on Cosgrove, clearly more susceptible to a sales pitch, which was, in reality, aimed at Leitch, the man who would have the final say. 'We're all in the same boat here. You and me. Working-class men.' He took a deep breath to allow his words to register. 'And when was the last time you enjoyed yourself? Had a bevvy? Met some new people?'

He paused once more as he detected a chink in the armour of his fellow soldiers. 'Come on, lads. It'll be a day to remember. You'll love the atmosphere at the match. And it'll give me a chance to see my son. He'll be back from his granny's after the game. Bridget's got it all arranged. If you take me away now and stick me in a cell, I won't get to see him. Bert, you'd feel just the same if you were in my shoes.'

Bridget had given no indication she'd been lugging into the conversation as she prepared a Lochee luncheon. Stephen snatched a sandwich before the plate on which they were placed had even touched the table.

'Do you have family, sergeant?' Bridget's query was genuine and Frank latched on to the possibility that the man sitting opposite may have something resembling a heart. Bridget was keen to know at least something of Leitch's background, but he was economical with the details of his back story. He had a son and a daughter, he told her. That would be enough for now. The famished threesome had a pressing priority - sandwiches to swallow.

Was it the food and strong tea that helped persuade the sergeant to reveal more? His wife, Ivy, he said, was also a mill worker. Bradford was a key centre for the production of various textiles. 'So, pretty much the same as Dundee.' He kept it brief, unwilling to offer further intelligence of his family life. He was a reluctant soldier, he confessed, and there, in Lochee, simply to carry out his task.

'Your husband's right,' he said to his hostess. 'Unfortunately, we don't know the destination of that boat he says we're all in. Mind you, he thinks he's unique and wants to bail out.'

Leitch was a solid, steady man in his mid-thirties, similar in age to McGarrity. He was highly regarded by his superiors as someone who could be depended on to do his duty. They were confident he would never waver when asked to do a job, no matter how heavy the responsibility. He was essentially a private person and did not, for instance, speak of the shrapnel wounds he had sustained in the Fall of France in June 1940 when the Auxiliary Military Pioneer Corps had been pressed into action as combat troops before being evacuated. In November that year the words auxiliary and military were dropped and the regiment was rebranded simply as the Pioneer Corps. Leitch's concern, he told Bridget, was nothing greater than that his wife and children remained safe from harm.

This blunt serviceman from Bradford continued to direct his conversation at the woman pouring him tea. 'Anyway, that's by the by.' He nodded towards Frank. 'All I have to do now is get this bugger back.'

Even Frank laughed, but thought he and his plan had been out of the picture long enough. So, like an impatient child with some important news that can't wait, he butted in.

'Of course, the alternative to the pub and the football,' he argued, 'is pretty good. Me in a police cell – I can handle that – and you two sitting on a hard bench for hours with your arses going numb.'

Bridget guessed what the topic up for discussion had been while she was shopping and meeting Harry; Frank giving Leitch earache in the hope his plan would be met by agreement. By this point, she was indifferent about the whole affair as long as Frank returned to see John, whom she would collect from her parents. She reminded him of that obligation. Just in case.

Cosgrove piped up. 'He's got something there, sarge. It's worth thinking about.'

'Don't be so bloody gullible, lad,' Leitch replied in his thick Yorkshire accent. 'We go for a few drinks, then what? Our prisoner needs a piss in the pub or at the match and disappears. How would we explain that? Or rather, how would *I* explain that? It would be my neck on the line.'

It was time for Frank's final, all or nothing, push. He fixed his eyes on the only man in the room who mattered and with a deep breath he mobilised his most sincere voice and donned the expression of a politician about to make a promise to the electorate. 'Listen, you've got nothing to worry about. You have my word. I won't let you down. I've nowhere else to go. There's my hand on it.'

The interminable pummelling from Frank on this topic made Leitch feel he was almost boxed into a corner. He looked at the outstretched hand then into Frank's eyes. Several seconds passed as the piano-wire tension built. Cosgrove bit his bottom lip. His eyes jumped between the protagonists in anticipation. The sergeant had to convince himself that he would always be in control.

But what if McGarrity did manage to escape my clutches? The consequences would be enormous. Come on, Bert, surely you wouldn't allow a mug like him to slip through your fingers. And anyway, when was the last time you enjoyed yourself? You're hundreds of miles from camp; hundreds of miles from a commanding officer. What harm could a couple of drinks and watching a local football match do?

Leitch had reached a decision. He took Frank's hand and pulled it and the rest of his body across the table. In a hushed but firm voice he said: 'One wrong step and I'll screw you into the ground; I swear.'

An accord of sorts was reached. Bridget knew it was only a matter of minutes before they would be off to the Nine Bells and that Frank would be tapping her for money.

11

Bridget intended to savour the luxury of being alone after her life had been disrupted by Frank's unexpected appearance the previous night. For two years she had made her own decisions, chosen her own path. She and John felt as settled as was possible in such impossibly difficult times. Any prolonged presence by Frank would have muddied the waters, interrupt her infidelity; bring her whole world crashing down. The routines were her routines. Everything was in its place. Her son enjoyed school and was doing well at his reading, writing and sums. She had high hopes for him, an apprenticeship perhaps, when he would leave St Mary's five years on, when he was fourteen.

She had the support of her mother. Her father's attitude was different. He did not stand in the way of such maternal succour, however. His relationship with his daughter had been strained since the emergence of Harry Lewis. There were few secrets in Lochee, certainly none in the Gallacher household.

Bridget and Frank's marriage had been one of convenience. Love and respect were never in the equation. That one night of overwhelming lust – Frank's - in a darkened close a decade earlier had produced the one gift she cherished, John.

But it brought embarrassment to her family, devout Lochee Catholics who held their heads high despite the disapproving looks and the finger pointing of neighbours and the clutch of hypocrites at chapel for Sunday Mass. Even the kind and tolerant Father Butler took some persuading to marry the unlikely couple with the six-year age difference before he surrendered to the pleas of Elsie Gallacher, Bridget's doting mother and a pillar of the Union of Catholic Mothers. Predictably, Monsignor Kearney had adopted the stand of a fundamentalist. No amount of begging for him to conduct the ceremony would have persuaded him to declare the couple husband and wife.

Frank's absence for nearly two years made life easier – and better - for Bridget. Gone were the bullying and the black eyes and bruised jaws that too frequently accompanied his drunken belligerence within the confines of the marital home. Bridget was an easy target and on the occasions news of his outbursts reached the Gallachers, immediate retribution was swiftly delivered by Bridget's male siblings, Brendan and Seamus, especially when she could not hide the marks Frank left on her pretty face with its high cheekbones and strong jawline. But there were many more beatings than they knew of, ones she managed to conceal or disguise. Now, she was free of an unpredictable husband, one too often fuelled by alcohol bought with borrowed money or family cash removed from Bridget's purse or, frequently, from the gas meter. The Bank of Tipperary, he called it. His social life was a priority; *the* priority. His intemperance also meant his relationship with John was not as it should have been and when Frank joined the army, relief arrived and blessed 13a Atholl Street.

John, though, had more important matters on his mind, the kind every nine-year-old prioritised; football, pals, fun, school. An absent father was a memory that was fading rapidly for him. This special, happy, healthy boy was the sole positive outcome from the marriage.

Yet, Bridget's loneliness and the relentlessness of her job and of raising her child single-handedly were tangible. What had a 28-year-old mother, on her own, to look forward to? Was this *it*? Thirty and more years in the mill, growing old and watching her boy evolve into middle-age and keeping a family of his own on pitiful wages?

Her parents despised Frank. They saw him as a man who had taken advantage of their daughter and who had subsequently displayed little or no interest in her welfare. And they knew, long before war service beckoned, that he was a work-shy philanderer, with little more than a smidgen of responsibility or character. There were others, particularly colleagues in the Pioneer Corps, who did not necessarily recognise that Frank McGarrity.

Despite that, when Bridget started seeing Harry Lewis, it was a step too far for her father. Jim Gallacher was a rough diamond; proud, like all Tipperary men, of his Irish heritage. It had been bad enough having a daughter fall pregnant out of wedlock. Now, she had started seeing another man while married to a soldier at war. It was too much for this principled, if misguided, man to stomach. There was also the further, crushing blow for Jim; Lewis was a Protestant.

Bridget's deep love for the new man in her life – a 'proper man' she called him – was unshakable and was reciprocated a hundred times over by someone she felt had the ethics and temperament she wanted in a life partner. But where would their romance lead? How could they plan for a future they desperately wanted to spend together?

Their weekly trysts were wonderful and wondrous and helped Bridget get through each week until they could be together again. His embrace, the touch of his hands on her body, the lengthy kisses, the tight embraces where they could hear the pounding of the other's heart against their own; she savoured every second they were together.

This must be what they mean by love.

12

Millie Barton wiped down the counter in the Nine Bells. She was proud of that bar top and its sheen. Her customers believed her loving care for the long, highly polished wooden surface was an obsession, and sometimes they would deliberately spill a few drops of their beer on to it and bet on how many seconds it would take before she whipped the always-at-the-ready cloth off her shoulder to replenish a shine that would have had Dundee's finest French polishers drooling.

Millie, short and stocky and with her hair pulled back and held tightly in a bun, ran her pub with a rigour and organisation Joseph Goebbels would have admired. Her face rarely cracked a smile, certainly not at quips directed at her, and the zeal with which she oversaw her establishment, made her a fearsome character. She ignored the jibes, but stored them in her memory until she decided the jokers who tossed them in her direction had overstepped the mark. Then, she would come down on them like a ton of bricks.

'Right, smart Alec,' she would rasp, 'you're barred.'

But her customers quite liked her ability to deal with the wisecracks as well as those tricky drinkers she judged had overstayed their welcome. She was shrewd enough, too, to recognise that taking someone down a peg or two was as much a cabaret for those customers not in the firing line as it was a warning that the offenders ought not to become over familiar with her. She also appreciated that tales of how she 'sorted out' this man, or that, gave her a kind of cache in Lochee and in other parts of Dundee.

Hughie McDonald was her right-hand man. Some of the regulars were convinced he was more than that, though they dared not mention so in front of Millie for fear of verbal retribution or worse, banishment from their favourite drinking den. But the idle speculation over whether the hard-faced businesswoman with her school mistress hairstyle, farmer's arms and breasts so heavy they sank to almost waist level, still had 'needs', provoked laughter among the men. Were that the case, they doubted whether Hughie could fulfil any duties in the bedroom department. He had the build of a whippet with black hair, heavy with Brylcreem, parted down the middle and combed back like William Powell. The slim moustache was another hint that he modelled himself on the Hollywood actor. Hughie could certainly claim to be The Thin Man, the title of one of Powell's hit movies. Drinkers referred to him as 'the fighting kirby grip' and reckoned he could not have weighed much more than nine stone, soaking wet. With his long white apron and stiff shirt collar, he assumed the appearance of an efficient barman. Such competence, however, was often disputed among the clientele.

Hughie had never married, but had been at Millie's side as long as anyone could remember and was brow-beaten like a timid border collie. Hen-pecked, they called him, despite such a term being reserved for husbands who were under the thumbs of dominant wives. Hughie was, indeed, the passive member of this double act - Stan Laurel to Millie's Oliver Hardy - and nobody had the definitive answer to the question of whether she had ever entered into matrimony. Was there a previous husband out there? It was an unsolved riddle.

The tightly-packed pub, with its low ceiling yellowed by decades of tobacco smoke drifting skywards and creating a cloudscape, caught the backs of the throats of any rare non-smokers who entered. The place hosted several regulars on this particular Saturday lunchtime. Among them were Gerald Murphy and Norman Hughes, old pals who had kept up their friendship from schooldays. They sat at a table to the left of the bar playing dominoes and trying from time to time to tease Neep Simpson about his long-past career in junior football,

The country's national sport was always the number one talking point among drinkers, even though the leagues had been suspended since the outbreak of World War II on September 1, 1939.

Nonetheless, while the possibility of Scotland beating England in an international match at Hampden Park that day came up for discussion, it was the Harp against the Violet that was the principal topic to spark debate and argument and, sometimes, ill-feeling.

Millie would often be required to intervene when quarrels boiled over. As soon as the temperature showed signs of rising during a dispute about the merits of one team or the other, her voice, throaty and deeper than seemed right for a woman, would boom out from behind the bar.

'That's enough. Any more of your nonsense and you'll be out on your arse,' she would bark to restore relative order.

Hughie, a scrawny weakling – like the 'before' model in one of the newspaper advertisements to encourage puny men to follow the Charles Atlas method of building their bodies - was less than sincere when showing an interest in Lochee's premier sporting event in an attempt to encourage Neep Simpson to participate in the discourse.

'I'm surprised you're not going to the game today,' he said, 'you being an ex-Violet man and all.'

Neep, grumpy and, as always, seated on his own at a small circular marble-topped table, growled something about the game being of no interest to him. Football wasn't as good as it was in his day, he insisted. 'A bunch o' Jessies,' was how he categorised the current crop of players. 'No hard men any more. Standards have dropped.'

It was the typical 'they're not as good as they were in my day' case put forward by former sportsmen.

The clear impression was that when he was performing for the Violet at the grounds of teams like East Craigie, North End and Stobswell, those who pulled on strips were tougher in the tackle and never complained when they were on the receiving end of a crunching challenge. To underscore his argument, he cited incidents of broken legs, displaced knee-caps and cut heads where there were no complaints from victims.

'Still,' Hughie continued, 'it's the Harp and the Violet, Neep. I thought that's at least one game you'd want to see.'

'I played nearly thirty years ago when players were players,' Neep harrumphed. This crabbit man, still in his fifties but regarded as 'old' would not be humoured.

Hughie saw it almost as his duty as 'assistant manager' – a title he bestowed on himself when meeting strangers who did not know any different - to lift spirits and create a happy atmosphere in the Nine Bells. 'You might actually enjoy it.'

'I don't enjoy enjoyment,' Neep responded. 'The last thing I went to was Jim Brady's fight at Tannadice on New Year's Day. I couldn't have been thinking straight. I mean, who'd pay good money to go and see two boxers in action in a football ground in the freezing cold?'

Heads rose in unison and looks were exchanged at that last remark.

'You *paid*?' Hughie was as astonished as the others at the thought that Lochee's meanest man had forked out for anything other than his pipe tobacco and beer.

'Well, I never actually paid,' Neep admitted rather sheepishly. 'Brady got me in for nothing. But what about the people who *did* pay? How daft were *they*? And how stupid was Kid Tanner to agree to a fight against a Scotsman, in Scotland, in sub-zero temperatures – *outside*? I mean, what was going through his head when his manager put his arm around him and said: "Come here Kid; I've got a great deal for you. You're going fight for the vacant British Empire bantamweight championship against a guy from Dundee, *in* Dundee, in the open air. And, here's the best bit, Kid, the temperatures will freeze your balls off. But it'll be fine." Fuck's sake, Tanner's from British Guyana. It's boiling there. The poor bastard was lucky he never died of the cold. *I* nearly died of it and I had a coat and a scarf and my bunnet on. All he had on were a wee pair of skimpy shorts.'

'And gloves,' was Norman's contribution, before adding: 'Okay, they were boxing gloves, but still … Oh, and by the way, Brady and Tanner have even got the same manager. He's picking up his percentage from both of them.'

The discussion over the dubious nature of the fight game came to a sudden conclusion as the pub door swung open and in walked Gino Esposito. Small in stature, wizened and frail-looking, he owned an ice cream parlour on South Road, right next door to the Nine Bells.

Gino was often the source of amusement for his fellow drinkers because of his broken English-cum-Lochee language delivery.

The door had barely swung closed behind him when he placed his order, asking Hughie to 'gies a pinta, please'. He shuffled his way to the bar, handed over nine pence and held up his drink for inspection. Was it cloudy or flawed in some other way? It wasn't. Had it too much of a head, one of Hughie's trademarks when pouring a pint of beer? It hadn't. 'Buona salute!'

He took his first sip before making an announcement. He always had some piece of news, plucked from customers or from passers-by as he stood in the doorway of his shop. And he knew how to achieve the greatest impact. 'So.' He took a second sip and held his pause as the bar came to attention. 'Have-a you heard aboot-a Frank McGarrity?' A longer gulp this time.

He now had the full attention of Millie and her customers. An impatient Gerald shouted: 'Would you get on with it.'

Gino placed his drink on Millie's pride and joy. 'He's a-hame.'

A communal murmur reverberated around the room. Jaws dropped. Except for Neep's. He appeared uninterested in whatever else Gino had up his sleeve.

He came a-hame. Last-a night. Unexpected.' Gino spoke slowly. He took another drink of his beer and waited for a response.

Neep suddenly perked up. 'That's a pity. I thought you were away to tell us news that a German sniper had got him.' He thought for a moment. 'You know what that means, don't you? He'll be in here soon enough and telling us how he's winning the war on his own. And you'd better watch out, Gino. We're fighting your lot as well. He might just go for you.'

Gino failed to see the funny side of that last remark. He thought for a moment, placed his drink on the counter as Millie hovered with her damp cloth in the event of spillage. 'Nah! I've-a done-a-ma' stint in the camp. You mind? Isle o' Man. Six-a months last year, when Mussolini, he decide to come into the war. Bastardo!' Another sip. 'I'm a Scottish noo. I'm on-a your side.'

It was like firing a starting pistol for the fun to start. Aside from Millie, everyone in the bar took the view that the gloves were off. Ridicule and derision were ramped up.

'You say you're Scottish, Gino,' Hughie chipped in, 'but can we trust you? I mean, how do we know your cones aren't laced with arsenic; that you're not an agent with orders to wipe out the population of Lochee, or at least the ones that prefer Grossi's ice cream to yours?'

The old Italian derided the observation and shook his head, but still felt the need to make his case. 'Ach, You're affa your bloody heid. My ice cream is-a far better than Grossi's. A'body kens that.'

The mood changed quickly, however. There were thoughts that a visit from McGarrity was inevitable, imminent even. This was a man who was not universally popular. He hogged conversations and sought to produce better, more exciting, funnier and hugely embellished tales than anyone else in the place. One-upmanship was his stock in trade. There was an air of acceptance that his appearance might just be minutes away and that a visit to Beechwood Park would be high on his agenda. It was inconceivable that he would be able to resist holding court before the football match, assuming he was aware that the Harp was playing the Violet a little later.

Someone asked if Gino had further information. Had he actually seen McGarrity?

'No,' he replied emphatically, 'but I was-a telt there were twa people up at his hoose. They had-a been at Bell Street first. To see the polis. I was-a thinking it might have been something to dae wi' the time before he left, when he was fightin' in-a the street.' He proceeded to remind his audience of an altercation in the Polepark area of Dundee. 'You mind? He telt a'body that he wrapped-a that-a Pole roond-a pole in-a Polepark, across fae Mitchell Street school. He was-a lucky he got awa' to the army or he would have got-a the jail.'

It was a more plausible reason of why Frank had joined up so quickly and more acceptable that his own story, that he felt it his duty to fight for his country.

'He was Ukrainian,' Neep muttered as he held his beer at his mouth in readiness for a drink.

'What-a are you on aboot?' Gino wasn't the only one puzzled by Neep's input.

'The Pole in Polepark. He was a Ukrainian.'

Gino shrugged his shoulders as if to show he either didn't know what Neep was talking about or that he couldn't care less, that such detail did not diminish his tale. It was equally possible that he ignored the comment on the basis that it ruined the alliteration in his little anecdote. He was astute enough to know what worked and what didn't when it came to storytelling. 'Aye, well-a, whatever. Onywy, aboot-a the twa men up at McGarrity's hoose.' He took a long, lingering drink as the assembled audience waited ... and waited. 'Sojers,' he said, finally.

'Sojers?' Neep sat up straight. Suddenly, he was interested. 'Maybe they're on a secret mission to blitz your ice cream shop with a couple of mortars, Gino.' Nobody laughed. Neep wasn't good at banter.

'Or maybe they'll drop a couple of grenades down Nessie Tennant's knickers,' Hughie joined in. 'Timed to go off when she goes for her famous morning visit to the lavvy in Cox's, the visit that prevents other women going in for about an hour after, till the smell dies down.'

Millie glared at him, unable or perhaps unwilling to acknowledge her assistant's comedic qualities, or lack of them.

Gino thought for a second or two. 'Naw, Nessie would just-a need to brack-a the wind as usual to bla' up the whole bloody mill. The Germans would gie her the Iron Cross to pin on her iron erse.'

The quips were underway, one drinker keen to outdo the one before.

'You're not wrong there, Gino.' It was Norman's turn to chip-in, taking a moment to look up from his double six in the domino match with Gerald. 'Nessie's a big woman. That would be a helluva fart. I don't know how wee Willie manages to keep her happy. It's like Benny Lynch squaring up to Primo Carnera.'

The mumbles in the bar told of agreement from customers as they pictured the world eight-stone champion Scot against the so-called Ambling Alp from Italy who stood 6ft 5ins tall and weighed-in at 18 stone 12 pounds.

Norman continued: 'You mind at the Locarno when they were courting and Willie would snuggle-up to her on the dance floor, his wee face buried into her enormous chest?' He looked apprehensively at Millie, expecting a rebuke. None came. 'It was always a waste of time trying to attract Willie's attention. It was a silent world in there.'

Norman's input to the comic element of the discussion brought nothing more than unified shakes of the head and a huge sigh from Neep.

'Is that the best you can do?' the former Violet player asked. 'You're about as funny as that Tommy Handley on the wireless, and that's not funny at all.'

No sooner had those words left Neep's lips and Norman and Gerald had once more turned their attention to their dominoes, than the pub doors flew open.

Like Athos, Aramis and Porthos they burst into the bar. The Three Musketeers sought refreshment. Frank certainly felt like he deserved reward for his tenacity and determination in bringing about a successful conclusion to his countless efforts to corrupt Leitch and guide him through a day of Lochee pleasure of the alcoholic and sporting varieties.

A momentary hush descended on the Nine Bells before Frank called on Millie to serve three pints of her best beer adding a disclaimer that he was pessimistic over what affect it would have on the youngest of the trio. 'That's half a pint to fill up each leg,' he said to Cosgrove.

It broke a certain strain as the other customers chortled while the private smiled. He wasn't altogether pleased, however, at being a figure of fun, especially in front of strangers.

'This is Stephen,' McGarrity introduced him to the assembly. 'He's young and not used to strong beer. So, we might have to keep an eye on him, in case he can't handle it.'

The room fell silent. The windbag was, indeed, in situ.

'We heard you were back,' said Hughie. Frank ignored him, looked around to see who was in the bar and introduced his other companion. They were fellow soldiers from the Pioneer Corps, he informed the customers, before going pointing out to his guests who was who.

'What's been happening, then?' Frank's question was put out there for anybody to answer. Somebody mentioned Jim Brady's winning fight at Dundee United's football ground a few months earlier. Frank had read that news, he revealed. 'Aye, somebody told me Scott of the Antarctic was in Brady's corner that night.'

Gino joined in. 'The boxers; they were-a shivering. There was snow on-a the ground. Neep was there, hoping one of the boxers would take a dive or drap-a doon deid; just to get it a' ower wi'. But it went-a the distance. Fifteen, long, boring, bollock-freezin' rounds. Neep said it was-a the first time he'd seen a black man turnin' blue. Is that no' right, Neep?'

It brought a roar of laughter; not from Neep.

Stephen had already consumed much of his beer in a series of large gulps. He admitted, albeit to himself, that it was, indeed, powerful stuff, but he liked it, and the scenario was all he could wish for.

Alcohol, new people to meet in what for him was a foreign land, and in the company of the man he looked up to more than any other, Private Frank McGarrity.

'It's an unusual name that,' Stephen turned to the quiet, lonesome, scowling man at a table on his own. 'Neep. Is that Scottish?' he asked innocently, jumping-in with both feet.

'Oh it's Scottish all right.' It was Frank's quick-as-a-flash cue for some additional merriment, as long as it was at somebody else's expense. 'Isn't it Neep? You see, Stephen, in Scotland, the word Neep is another name for a turnip.' He pushed out his arm theatrically towards Neep. 'See the resemblance? I mean, look at the size of that head. But, to give him his due, that man scored more goals with his napper than any other player in Dundee junior football. Right, Neep?'

Neither Stephen nor Leitch, still arguing with himself over whether it was right to sanction the extension of freedom he afforded his prisoner, were unsure whether to laugh or simply spare Neep's blushes by turning a deaf ear to Frank's wisecrack, designed to taunt his long-time verbal sparring partner. They chose the latter option.

Neep, his frayed, well-worn grey tweed cap on the table beside his beer, was not displeased by McGarrity's description of his goal-scoring exploits during his prime, though not by what had preceded it on the issue of the size of his head, which was frequently a regular theme in conversations in the bars of Lochee and elsewhere in Dundee.

Had he been born with an unusually big bonce? Had he come from a family of people with enormous domes? He'd heard all the jokes before about its circumference and how two normal-sized heads would fit into his cap, not to say that there was no neck in evidence between his head and shoulders. It had been forced downwards by all that heading of the leather ball, often made heavier with mud and rain. There were those who actually believed such a theory.

'Double figures with my head every season,' Neep affirmed. 'I once scored sixteen in a season,' he added proudly from his seated position and he nodded his head violently to illustrate his prowess. 'All with the nut and many more with my feet.'

Frank was invited by a rather subdued Millie to dig into his pocket and produce the two shillings and three pence for the drinks he'd ordered as he inquired of Gino how well his ice cream business was doing. Not that he was particularly interested. It was simply for something to say; to hear his own voice.

The little Italian outlined the hardship he suffered in those troubled times. Cones were still selling reasonably well, he reported, especially at weekends after 12 o'clock Sunday Mass when the centre of Lochee became more populated for a short time.

McGarrity didn't reckon on a full run-down of the popularity or otherwise of Gino's products, but he was given it anyway. Sliders were decent sellers, but there was no market for chocolate wafers or squashers because they were rationed. In any case, the Italian pointed out, they would be unaffordable, even for the most discerning of Lochee's gelato lovers.

Leitch and Cosgrove glanced at each other as if to say: 'What the hell are they talking about?'

'So, I'm just aboot-a keeping my heid fae goin' under the water,' Gino continued. 'Onywy, money's no' important. It's-a your health that-a coonts. Me? I'm-a gettin' bather wi' my liver.' He was on to another of his favourite subjects; his health.

'I tak-a the Carter's liver pills for it. They say it gies you-a vim and-a vigour. But no' for me, it disnae.'

'Neep's clearly not full of vim and vigour either,' Frank broke in, keen to draw the conversation away from news of Gino's ailments and their potential cures and back to himself. 'But he'll be full o' shite if he thinks the Violet'll win today.'

This was an in-at-the-deep-end introduction to Scottish badinage for the brace of soldiers from south of the border and Stephen expressed mild surprise at how seriously football was taken, prodding Frank to launch into yet another speech, starting with the importance of the game to the working class. And he chose that day's match to underline his favourite subject, the discrimination of Catholics.

He placed an arm around the shoulder of the rookie soldier, by now on his second pint of beer.

'It'll put hairs on your chest,' Millie told him.

The tutorial began. 'On the one hand, you've got the Violet. A bit better off than many of the other clubs. Full of blue noses – that's the Protestants, by the way – and they're always, always, desperate to beat us, the Harp, the Tims; the Catholics.'

Stephen smothered a yawn with a hand. Neep turned away and shook his head. 'How long have you got, lads?' he asked the soldiers sardonically. 'We've heard this a hundred times.'

Frank's stride would not be broken. This was Spencer Tracy in full flow in a Dundee dialect. 'History tells us that we are the downtrodden, the underdogs. The mugs brought in from places like Glasgow and farther afield like Ireland to man – or rather *woman* – the jute mills so that people like the Cox family can make their pile and live lives of luxury.'

Gino nodded his agreement and chipped-in. 'So, in a football context, these are-a the kind o' people who, if they were-a fitba' supporters, would support the Violet.'

The debate gathered pace. Leitch thought it didn't sound much like football, more like religious warfare, while Neep accused Frank and 'his lot' of being obsessed and choosing not to mention that the incomers of which he spoke were starving and had no work when they arrived. Why else had they 'immigrated' to Lochee?

'They needed to earn a living,' Neep continued. 'Feed their bairns. They're always making out they're hard-done by because they're Catholics. It's nothing to do with their religion. They were given jobs.'

He then proceeded to give a short, but not short enough for Frank, lesson on Dundee Violet to offer balance to the discussion. Their home ground of Glenesk Park was less than a mile from the Harp's, he started. They had won the Scottish Junior Cup twelve years earlier, the first club from the area to do so. They had defeated Denny Hibs 4–0 at Dundee FC's Dens Park after a second replay. Neep was proud to report those and other statistics about his former team that were embedded in his mind.

Leitch gave a reasonable impression of being interested in the history of two minor football clubs he had never heard of, but could not prevent his eyes from glazing over, nor his mind wandering to more personal matters, like his wife and children.

Still, there were parts of the picture being drawn of life in Lochee that enthralled him, if not Cosgrove, who constantly and nervously touched his side holster, checking it to satisfy himself that his Enfield No. 2 was still there. Carrying a pistol was a new experience for him and he felt a heavy responsibility at being entrusted with army property, let alone one that could kill. He and Leitch had been issued with their revolvers as 'regimental policeman' their temporary role for the purpose of delivering McGarrity to an army cell.

'Maybe you're right, Neep,' Frank retaliated. 'Maybe it's all in our imagination. Maybe I just dreamt that when I left school and went for a job as an apprentice mason – not your kind of mason, by the way – the man who interviewed me asked what church I went to. That was his second question after asking my name. He went through them all, all the Proddie churches in Lochee, that is. Strangely, he didn't mention St Mary's. It never crossed his mind. I was only about thirteen at the time. So, innocently, I explained my church was up towards the Rialto, just after the library and the swimming baths. He thought for a few seconds, and then it hit him. Like a fucking sledgehammer. The smoke from his pipe billowed faster. I swear it was coming out his ears as well. He stopped puffing his bogey roll, looked me straight in the eye as I stood, shaking like a leaf, on the other side of his desk. "The *Catholic* Church?" he shouted. "You're a *Pape*?" His neck was bulging, his face turned red, then purple. I've never seen anybody having a heart attack, but I think he was on the verge of one. "Get the fuck out of my office," he yelled. "There'll be no Catholics working here".'

Stephen, now edging towards the slurring stage, had disbelief writ large across his face as he expunged the beer's froth from his mouth. 'Are you saying you couldn't get a job because of your religion?'

'That's the reality of life here, son,' Frank explained. 'And that's why we want to see the Harp winning today. It's our little way of getting back at the bastards. And here's another thing. Do you not think it's strange that there are no Celtic players in the Scotland team against England today?'

Gino could see the way the wind was blowing, one that brought bitterness with it, and laid out his credentials for entry into the diplomatic service. Unfortunately, he deployed words his audience had trouble deciphering. 'So, what does it-a matter? You're a' stupid. Could it no' just-a mean the Celtic players are no' good enough?'

Millie, always listening into the conversation, just in case her chucking-out talents were called upon, wiped with an urgency the surfaces she had already rubbed a dozen times since opening time.

Hughie had both feet firmly in his mouth when he said: 'I don't care who's in the team as long as they hammer those English basta …' He pulled up short, remembering the new pub guests and their country of birth. 'Sorry lads. No offence.'

The apology was too late to prevent the thwack of Millie's wet cloth across the back of his head. 'Change the barrel, you eejit,' she commanded as he slinked off to the cellar.

Leitch waved his hand, signalling that no umbrage had been taken and he began to entertain the idea that McGarrity's call for a pre-match drink was not as bad a suggestion as he initially feared. It was quite fun, compelling almost, despite the potency of the crossfire.

Gino was similarly minded. He extended his stay at the Nine Bells because he didn't want to miss anything he could relay first-hand to his customers. Mrs Esposito would have to hold the fort at the unimaginatively-named, Gino's Ice Cream Parlour, for a little longer.

The small-in-stature Italian was also enjoying the attention he was receiving and was keen to participate in the comedy-drama that was playing out. The silence that followed Hughie's little faux pas allowed him to inject another line. 'They're a' daft; Catholics, Proddies. Who cares? Where I come fae they're a' Tims and still they fight among themselves. So, this thing aboot-a religion, it's just an excuse for aggravation and argument. They love it. Both sides.'

Neep, eager to redirect the discourse on to saner ground, turned his attention to more mundane issues as he peppered the English guests with questions about themselves; where they were from, what they did as jobs before signing-up for military duty, did they have families? It was all the kind of data in which Frank had shown no interest, mainly because it ate up valuable minutes when he could be hearing his own voice.

Leitch explained that he felt obliged to join up, despite being in a reserved occupation as a coal miner. He thought he would be better off in the Pioneer Corps than stuck hundreds of feet down a mine.

'Mind you,' he said, 'the jobs have a lot in common. You dig - I've forgotten how many miles of trenches we've done - you get filthy, you work in teams; you dice with death. We've seen plenty of horror, all three of us, that we'd rather not have witnessed. God knows, nobody wants this war. I look at young lads like Stephen, and I worry. Twenty-two-years-old. He should be enjoying himself instead of wondering if he's going to be hurt, or worse. What kind of future can *he* plan for?'

Frank, listening to Leitch, signalled to Millie that three more drinks were needed. Then, he turned to the sergeant. 'I never thought you felt so strongly; about the war, I mean. You sound like you're against it.'

Leitch was a cool character who could articulate his views in a clear fashion, without wishing to be the centre of attention. 'That's pretty daft,' he said. 'Nobody in their right mind would be for war, would they? Maybe you haven't been hearing to me.

Then again, you're not famous for listening, are you? Certainly not to anybody in authority.'

'Aye, okay. But a sergeant? Well, that's not *real* authority. Is it? You're just one of the lads. Except when you're being a bit of a pain in the neck. Which is quite often. Agreed?'

Leitch took the insult on the chin and in the fun way it was intended. 'Yeah, well, it's my job. Can you not see that? What kind of army do you think we'd have if it was down to people like you? I'd be coming to you and saying: "Excuse me, Mr McGarrity, but there are dead and wounded bodies out there. Would you mind helping to bring them back?" I loathe what we have to do, but it's the hand we've been dealt and all the political arguments and soap-box speeches in the world won't change it. That'll be done at the ballot box when the war's over. But, if that evil bastard Hitler wins, he'll be dishing out the orders. Not me. That's why we have to put our faith in Churchill.'

Leitch was unaware that Winston Churchill's name was mud in Dundee where he was seen as an enemy of the people.

'How can you stick up for Churchill? And you a miner?' McGarrity could not understand the sergeant's logic.

Suddenly, this was two men of a similar age and background and with much in common, beginning to discover their similarities. It had never occurred to Frank before. He had seen Leitch as a kind of adversary, like they weren't on the same side.

The miner from Bradford pushed his point. 'Churchill's the best we've got. He's the leader. And we're at war. But when the war's over, that's when we'll wage our own battle, against the Tories and all they stand for.'

'Aye, well, you're behind the times, pal. We dumped Churchill as our MP twenty years ago, when he was a Liberal. Tried to get re-elected. Came fourth. That's how much we rated him. And the best bit was that he was beaten by a prohibitionist. Can you imagine that? Ed Scrymgeor, an anti-drink campaigner, elected to a seat in Dundee where everybody likes a drink? Churchill couldn't believe it.'

Agreement rumbled around the room like bees buzzing at a rose bush, but they were swiftly halted when McGarrity

86

glanced at the clock behind the bar. 'Shite! Look at the time.' He swallowed the remainder of his beer and urged his companions to follow suit. 'We'd better get going or we'll miss the kick-off.'

Stephen, unsteady on his feet and struggling to finish his drink, still couldn't bring himself to leave the inch of aler left in his glass. He wiped his mouth with the back of his hand and emitted one long, loud burp. 'Fucking hell,' he said as he checked his pistol yet again, 'that beer is bloody strong,'

14

The quiet tap on the door was followed by the slow turn of the handle; Harry, perspiring and out of breath, stepped into 13a. Bridget was shocked and scared. She panicked. Hadn't she warned him that Frank would be there?

The Saturday evening ritual, those precious hours that were the key to the evolution of their love for each other, had been cancelled, she reminded him with a mixture of fear and anger. What if Frank had been home?

Bridget's mother was a willing party to the weekly arrangement, hence John's regular weekends with his granny and granddad, although Jim Gallacher pretended to be unaware of the real reason his grandson was with them from Friday nights to Sunday lunchtime. It was after Mass and its long, tedious sermon from Monsignor Kearney that John was returned to Tipperary, which at least meant Harry did not have to scurry away from 13a too early. It did not prevent eyes being trained on him, though, as neighbours put two and two together to ascertain what was happening.

Jim would never condone his daughter taking up with another man – let alone a Protestant man – while she was still married, despite the unhappiness Frank brought her. She had made her bed, she could lie in it, was his view. At one family gathering soon after her husband joined the army, he let slip that the best thing that could happen for his daughter and her son was that McGarrity fell to a German bullet. There was a gasp here and there from the women in the family at the time, but secretly they agreed with him.

Bridget was flustered, on edge and a little displeased as she reiterated to Harry why he could not stay. In turn, he tried to give her peace of mind, a mind in turmoil. He explained he had listened at the door for voices before entering. The quiet told him she was alone. It was not yet half past five and she had been sick with anxiety since the moment Frank had crossed the threshold the previous night.

'I didn't want you to be on your own,' Harry said as he slipped his hands round her tiny waist. 'I know he's a violent man, especially with drink in him. That's what you've told me. I came to support you; to protect you.'

They hugged, long hugs, almost squeezing the life from each other. They kissed and stared into each other's eyes as Harry promised he would love her until his last breath. Nothing and no-one mattered more.

'You can't stay,' she told him. 'Go! He's due back. He promised he'd be here to see John.'

'John?' Harry was confused. He pulled back suddenly from her. Was John in the other room, or out playing and likely to barge in?

'It's fine,' she said. 'I was supposed to have John here to see his dad, but I couldn't be sure Frank would turn up and if he didn't, John would be crushed. I decided that whatever would come my way, I'd leave him with his gran and I've been praying Frank won't do the unexpected and come home; not when he's had a drink. John's seen enough of that over the years.'

Harry realised how fraught and difficult it was for her and how fragile she was in such circumstances. He sympathised that she was in an intolerable situation. He pulled her close, tried to ease her worries with encouraging words and told her that whatever happened, he would take care of her and her boy. She was not alone and never again would be, he assured her.

'I'll wait with you,' he said. 'We'll face this together. Maybe it's time for him to know. I'm here for you and John from now on.'

This may have brought a welcome speck of comfort to her, but the thought of a horrific, full-blown fight and its consequences, filled Bridget with trepidation. The palms of her hands were sweaty, her nerves frayed, her pulse throbbing so loud she could almost hear it.

Not for the first time, she talked about the shame that would engulf her family were she to leave Frank and take up with Harry, no matter how much the lovers wanted such a scenario. Her heart was bursting with joy every time she was with him, but it was a dream with a potential nightmare ending.

Happiness was her biggest wish, but the road towards it was strewn with the real possibility of mayhem and carnage and untold and lasting damage.

'We could leave and set up home far away from here,' Harry protested. 'There are jobs for schoolteachers all over the place. I respect that your family would be disappointed because of their religious beliefs, but please, Bridget, don't allow it to swallow you up. God knows how you've suffered with this man. You deserve better. I'd give anything just to have you with me for the rest of my life.'

'Get on your way,' she urged Harry, 'and if you meet him on the way, just walk past. Don't make eye contact.'

They kissed once more, a long, protracted meeting of moist lips. They held each other tightly. Harry cupped her weary face in his soft, tender hands, untroubled by manual labour, and reassured her that everything would work out well. Yet, as if Bridget were a magnet, he felt it almost impossible to step away from her. Their fingers touched as he left. His heart was heavy, but he was ready, should he come face to face with the man he had replaced in Bridget's life, to confront him. By the time he reached the end of the row of houses and turned into St Ann's Street, however, no military men were sighted.

15

Hughie opened the Nine Bells for the ever-thirsty evening boozers on the stroke of five. Millie, in her fresh Saturday night finery, a crisp white blouse, a touch of make-up and the most vivid of red lipstick, was doing what Millie did best. If the bar top could have spoken it would have begged her to stop fussing over it. This was a landlady with great pride in her premises, one who would be 'polisher of the year' that and every subsequent year were there such an award to be contested. Was that beeswax the customers could smell off her? Or had every odour simply been overpowered by her two-bob-a-gallon eau de Cologne from DM Brown's, her favourite department store in Dundee, as Lochee citizens referred to the city in which they lived, as if it were a separate entity.

No more than a few minutes passed before customers filtered into the pub, each wondering if there had been news of whether Scotland had beaten England at Hampden. Some looked forward to the paper boy arriving with the evening's Sporting Post and the important football results and reports it carried.

Neep made his way to his table, always left vacant for him to occupy. He growled a hello to Hughie, Millie and anybody else who heard his low-key greeting. His usual pint was delivered tout suite by the as-neat-as-ever barman. Hughie looked as if he and his apron had been freshly ironed. There may even have been a second coat of hair cream to weigh down his head and put additional pressure on his scrawny neck, too thin for a shirt collar that stuck out a couple of inches from his Adam's apple.

He kicked-off the conversation. 'You'll be wondering what the score is at Beechwood, eh Neep?'

'I'm thinking more about those poor soldiers,' he replied, 'and how they'll cope with the kind of place McGarrity's taken them to. Wait till they see that clown in action; hurling abuse at the referee and at the Violet players and their supporters. I just hope somebody puts their fist in his big mouth. That way we won't have to listen to his match summary when he comes in.'

Millie was in a conciliatory frame of mind and, in her weaker moments, viewed Frank as harmless, if over-opinionated and loud. Essentially, he wasn't a bad man, she exclaimed. Yet, even as she made her pro-McGarrity remarks, she doubted herself after being reminded of the stories of his fondness for lifting his hands to his wife. Few matters, even those that took place in the home, were secret in Tipperary. Frank might be all right, but not if you had to live with him, she thought, or be on the end of the tyrannical side of his nature.

It sparked judgements of McGarrity from Neep that were jaundiced and acerbic. They were opinions rooted in years of a deep hatred between the two with neither ready to accept the sentiments of the other on any subject matter. McGarrity was a bad egg, Neep declared, a waster who believed he could drift through life without a care in the world.

'There are probably a few more like him in the Pioneer Corps,' he added, unfairly, some thought. 'I mean, what kind of regiment is it anyway? It's got Czechs, Austrians and Poles in it, and Christ knows what else. It's even got Germans.'

'Germans?' said Hughie, thinking Neep had been mistaken. 'How can it have Germans?'

'They're Germans who've been living here.' came the reply.

'But they're still Germans. I can't understand it; how can they fight against their own country?'

Millie seemed to know something of the matter at hand. 'Thousands of them joined the Pioneer Corps because they wanted to free their country from the Nazis,' she explained. 'It was the same with the Austrians already over here. They wanted the Huns out of *their* country. Our government calls them friendly aliens.'

Suddenly, the door burst open with a bang and bounced off the wall. The three Pioneers had covered their two-mile walk from Beechwood Park to where Bank Street ended and South Road began - the Nine Bells entrance - in record time, marching some of the way, staggering the rest. There was a determination that precious drinking time would not be squandered while

McGarrity's meeting with his boy seemed, at least for the moment, to slip his mind.

By now, they were comfortable enough with each other to be on first name terms. Rank was put aside and they appeared to have forgotten one of them was a prisoner. Not enough, however, to stop Stephen from constantly patting his holster anxiously. Checking and double checking ... then checking again.

'It's still there,' Frank teased. 'Don't worry about it. You'll not be shooting anybody today.'

Leitch picked up the tab for the three pints Frank ordered as they approached the bar and, pressed by the sergeant, accepted it would be just one drink then back to Tipperary to see John before departing Dundee, if not in handcuffs, then clearly as a re-captured runaway soldier.

The bar became busier, Norman and Gerald, known locally as 'Flanagan and Allen' after the English musical hall comedy duo nobody liked nor found funny, took up their usual position on a bench seat behind a small rectangular table while several others arrived after watching the Harp and the Violet.

Millie stopped polishing for a moment. 'Right!' She called the customers to attention. 'Get it out in the open so we can move on. What was the score?'

Frank swigged his beer and looked over at Neep. 'Two-one to the Harp.'

'Fuck!' Neep's breathy comment told the others what they already knew, that this was not what he wanted to hear. There would be no stopping McGarrity now. It would be a festival of gloating and a not so gentle rubbing of salt into wounds.

'Yes.' Frank made a sweeping gesture with his free hand and, for the entire clientele to hear and in the style of a Shakespearean actor with a thick Dundee accent, he added: 'A victory for good over evil, for right over wrong.' He strode towards Neep and leaned over his table. He clenched his fist in front of the enemy. 'And for Pape over Proddie.'

There was stifled laughter among some of the drinkers, the Catholic ones. Others did not take Frank seriously while two or three baulked at such inflammatory language in case blood as well as beer was spilled on Millie's teak bar.

Neep did not flinch. He stared right back at his foe. 'Piss off, you moron!'

The loud slap of Millie's hand on to her beloved counter turned heads. Her eyes were filled with fury. She slung her cloth over her shoulder and pointed at Frank. 'You! Buggerlugs! Keep a lid on it. You know the rules. No religious nonsense in here that's going to sail too close to the rocks. Got it?'

In two seconds, the anger tap was turned off. She cleaned the mark her palm had made on the bar and in an instant she was Mrs Pleasant. 'So lads,' she addressed the Englishmen, 'did you enjoy the match?'

Leitch admitted it was, indeed, a memorable occasion for a variety of reasons. The rugged-looking man from the West Riding rubbed his mop of dark wavy hair and revealed that his prisoner had created quite a stir among what he thought was a surprisingly-large crowd for a non-professional football match. He estimated it to be close to a thousand, maybe more, and that Frank had been at the centre of off-the-pitch action that, for a time, took the crowd's attention away from the actual game. A sideshow, he called it.

Leitch turned to McGarrity. 'What was it you were shouting about the referee, again? Something about him being in the same Masonic lodge as half the Violet team. That went down well, eh Frank?'

Stephen's demeanour, meanwhile, was Buster Keaton-like; glum and disconsolate. It was obvious he was struggling with Millie Barton's beer. He addressed Frank. 'Yeah. You were full of it, weren't you? That Violet supporter stirred it up, eh? Shouted it was time you were getting down the road to confession. To cleanse your green, white and gold soul, he said.'

The young private turned to his fellow customers as Leitch rolled his eyes. He painted a vivid picture of the events of that afternoon. 'So, he tries to get the fella by the throat. Me and the sarge pull him off the man. We've got an outstretched arm each and he's like Christ on the cross. Then, the Violet guy steps forward and he gives Frank a big, exaggerated blessing that set

94

off laughter among both sets of supporters. I'm sure some of the players were sniggering, too.'

'Aye, is that right? Well, it was just as well you stopped me getting at him,' a seething Frank argued. 'I'd have knocked him out.'

But Stephen, now with a boozer's bravado as he topped-up on his pre-match intake, was not prepared to let the matter rest. He questioned if the man he idolised when they were side by side in the regiment, could have handled the burly, growling, granite-faced Violet supporter.

'I know you *tell* us how good a fighter you are,' he said, before turning once more to the Nine Bells' drinkers, perhaps looking for confirmation, 'but has anybody actually seen him in a fight? Have you?' The audience remained silent, some too apprehensive to contribute to a conversation cocooned in controversy. 'No? Maybe you *are* a fantasist, then, Frank. That's what they were saying at the football.'

The large-headed, lionhearted loner at his own table chipped-in. 'I've been saying that for years,' he grumbled.

In an instant, the atmosphere began to turn as sour as out-of-date milk. Leitch made an attempt to bring peace and serenity to proceedings, but Frank was stung by Cosgrove's caustic observations.

He repeated his previous warning to Stephen that he was destined for defeat in his battle with Scottish beer and its potency. He teased the Cockney kid that he was not so much Popeye as Olive Oyl and cautioned him to slow down in his consumption.

Stephen once more tapped his holster as Gino arrived in search of grog and gossip. He was pleased to see Frank there with the hope that the wayward soldier would bring some Saturday evening entertainment, preferably bolstered by a punch-up.

Yes, a fight would be good, others might have concluded, especially if McGarrity did not emerge unscathed. Thoughts rumbled around the room that, with an outspoken Cosgrove, courageous courtesy of Millie's powerful sherbet, as the opposition, a square go could be in the offing. Given his wobbly legs, muddled mind and feeble body, though, the betting would be on the older soldier to emerge victorious.

Leitch cottoned-on quickly to the fresh and unwelcome friction between the boy-man and the colleague he once regarded as a paladin of the regiment. This was the youngster who had hitherto hung on Frank's every vainglorious word, laughed at all his corny jokes and swallowed every bumptious claim that came out of his mouth. McGarrity, the sergeant believed, may just have lost his number one admirer.

Gino's entry proved a diversion and released some of the tension that was beginning to build. Leitch was grateful for his intercession, though the little ice cream seller was oblivious to the fact that his arrival was so timely. The Nine Bells needed a distraction. Gino shuffled his way to the bar to stand alongside the soldiers. Now, however, with the liquor playing its part in proceedings, Leitch's worries increased over whether the mission he led would be completed without calamity.

A moustache of white froth covered Gino's top lip after his first, long, drouthy drink and an afternoon of slow trade in his shop. He wiped his mouth with an off-white skanky hankie, which hadn't seen Mrs Esposito's washboard for a long time, possibly since before the war. He pulled it from the breast pocket of his shiny dark jacket, part of Gino's dress code for as long as anyone had remembered. 'It's a wee bit-a chilly oot there, Millie,' he said. 'You would hardly think it was-a the start of May. It would freeze your-a brass monkeys aff.' He rubbed the backs of his scrawny hands from which a series of purple veins protruded. Then, with all the timing of a diplomat who just managed a pass mark in the exams for the foreign service, he remarked to no-one in particular that it was a 'good-a result for-a the Harp eh?' and followed this up with a appeasing glance to the forlorn drinker with the massive head. 'Nae offence, Neep.'

Gino had important news. He always did. There were two Violet supporters querying people in Bank Street as to what pub Frank drank in. He looked to the subject of that investigation. 'Shifty O'Flynn, he was in-a my shop and was-a telling me he'd been asked whaur-a you'd be. He telt them you'd be at-a your hoose, but that he didnae ken the address. They were angry, rough-looking bastards, he said.'

It prompted Frank and Leitch to simultaneously cast their eyes in the direction of the clock, each remembering the promise the wayward soldier had made to his Bridget, that he would be home directly after the match. That promise had already been broken.

Stephen had taken himself off to a chair beside Norman and Gerald. His head flopped forward and he flitted in and out of consciousness, wakening himself intermittently when the gas from the beer exploded inside him and caused him to rift with an unusually high decibel count.

'We've still got time,' Frank whispered to Leitch out of the side of his mouth. 'Best leave Rip Van Winkle for a wee while. He's out the game.'

He then focused on Gino. 'Shifty should have told the shrinking violets I'd be in here, Gino. We'd have seen how hard they are.'

Now keen to increase his intake of booze before his imminent departure, Lochee's self-proclaimed champion bare-knuckle fighter set his alcohol intake dial higher. He wished to reacquaint himself with John Barleycorn, a taste he had all but forgotten. 'Millie.' He raised his chin to summon the lady of the house. 'How about some of the hard stuff? To celebrate my homecoming - and my leaving.'

He clenched his teeth in anticipation of a barrage of abuse for being so presumptuous. Millie's jaw tightened and her lips once more disappeared into a thin line. She leaned across the bar to prevent others from hearing her admonishment. 'Come on now, Frank. Where would I get whisky? It's wartime.'

Frank dug deep into his reservoir of charm. He clasped her hand and, dropping his head and signalling with his eyes towards the counter, he speculated. 'Millie dear, I know you keep a couple of bottles of Bell's under there for your pals and your best customers. Please? Three half and halfs and if Sleeping Beauty over there doesn't wake up, I'll dispose of his.'

Millie pulled her hand away and with a steely glare through narrowed eyes she expressed a hope that he could pay for the

Scotch. No tick in her pub, she stressed. The rule was simple; drink now, pay now.

'Well, as luck would have it,' Frank divulged, 'my dear brother Tommy was at the match and made a very generous donation to my funds.'

The firewater was produced and the chatter continued while other drinkers licked their lips and looked on with envious eyes. Whisky, however, was outside the boundaries of their price bracket.

Meanwhile, Leitch was still quiet, keeping his own counsel. He was conscious of the tightness of the time needed to re-visit Tipperary and for McGarrity to see John before step one of their sojourn south – a tram journey to Lindsay Street - was taken.

The three soldiers had consumed much more alcohol than any of them had anticipated, each as inebriated as sailors after a night in port following weeks at sea. This was a big deal for them. They had not been within sniffing distance of jungle juice for a painfully long time. The strong Scottish beer had, however, taken its toll on Stephen significantly more than his older companions.

Frank began to ramble. He reflected on how Bridget had done him proud in raising John. His son was going to 'be someone' when he grew up, maybe even play for Celtic. The two of them were everything to him. Sentimentality and a false belief that all was well with his marriage, kicked-in.

Leitch labelled him lucky and he, too, sang the praises of his own wife and family. But there was little thought of making a move to Atholl Street. Each time it came up – fleetingly – in conversation, there was always the 'plenty of time' excuse for staying put.

A maudlin Frank attested that there was nothing to look forward to after the war, unless there was a change in the political landscape. 'No jobs. No opportunities. No bloody money. You know, I once had a headmaster who used to say that the two most important things in life were the grace of God … and money. Well, you can keep your grace of God, whatever that is; give me the cash every time.'

The sergeant, himself suitably lubricated, was more lucid than he had been previously, almost like a switch had been flicked in his brain to tell him he was past the point of no return and that he had permission to gibber. He felt Frank was too defeatist. No ambition, no initiative. 'You owe it to your wife and son to try harder. When this war is over, it will offer us all a fresh start.'

'Well, I am good with my hands.' Frank blew his own trumpet. Again.

'There you are, then. You can learn how to be a carpenter or a bricklayer. Wait you'll see. There'll be jobs in the construction trade when all this is over. They'll have to do something about rebuilding our towns and cities, especially the ones hit by bombs. We'll need housing, for a start. So, don't give up.'

They supped their ale in silence for a couple of minutes, each consumed by his own thoughts as they surveyed the busy bar and whether Stephen could be resuscitated.

'You're not such a bad bastard, are you?' Frank laughed.

'For a sergeant?' said Leitch.

'For an Englishman.'

16

There was agitation in the air. It didn't go unnoticed. Bridget's mind seemed to be elsewhere. Her elderly neighbour had grown tired of listening to Vera Lynn on the wireless - Nellie was one of the few residents of Tipperary who could afford one - and having watched the comings and goings on the outside stair throughout the day, like a spy from military intelligence, she surmised that the coast was clear for a trip across the landing.

Bridget was not naïve. She suspected that the 'friendly call' was as much to do with curiosity and cross-examination as it was about empathy.

'Where the buggery is he?' Bridget soliloquised. 'The swine's in the pub. Course he is.'

'The question is,' said Nellie, as if it were her business, 'where is he getting the money?'

'That's what I've been wondering.' Bridget ran that thought aloud through her mind then poured herself and her companion each a small sherry, leftovers from Hogmanay. She called it 'a comfort drink' and kept it for special occasions and this could, indeed, be deemed a special, although not necessarily a happy, one. 'I gave him half a crown. But how long will that last?'

Nellie was in her usual position in such situations, on the very top of the moral high ground. 'Well, wherever he got it, he'll be well-on by now.' She closed her eyes and turned her head to one side as if to emphasise her disgust. It was as though she was feeling offended on behalf of Bridget, but equally, she was keen to share her repugnance of Frank. Nellie sipped her Harvey's Bristol Cream and looked at the glass as if to check how much was left. It didn't take long for her nosiness to bubble to the surface. 'The men he's with. Is it true what they're saying about them?'

'Who's saying what about what men, Nellie?'

'It's just that … well, Nancy McKenzie …'

'Hah! I knew it! Nancy McKenzie, the mouth of the Tay. And what was it she was saying?' Bridget felt a surge of indignation. Being the centre of gossip among other women made her blood boil.

Nellie endeavoured to creep around a touchy issue. 'I'm just saying, Bridget. To put you on your guard, you know.'

But Bridget was keen for Nellie to spit it out, and to detail 'what was that scabby-faced yap McKenzie telling you?'

Nellie did her best to dampen a fire she feared could grow into a full-blown blaze, perhaps accompanied by raised voices. She knew she had to tread carefully, but she was desperate to get to the bottom of what had been going on. 'I can't right mind what she was saying. I was only half listening.'

'Is that right? And what half was that?' Bridget touched her right ear. 'Was it that half, with this ear?' She touched her other ear. 'Or was it that half with this one?'

'For God's sake, Bridget. I was in Ugly Boab's buying some margarine when she came in. I could hardly walk away, could I? She just blurted it out to everybody. Mary McPhee was there. Annie Duncan was in the queue. And Connie Moran. And Ugly Boab, of course; being as it's his shop.'

'Oh he'd have loved that; old sweetie wife,' was Bridget's scathing description of the unappealing shopkeeper. The rallies were now in full flow, almost unstoppable, but Bridget's observation of Ugly Boab was accurate. He was a bigger trader in titbits than any of his largely female clientele.

'He loved it all right,' Nellie confirmed. 'He said deserters should be shot. Went on about when he was in the First War and what happened to the men who refused to fight. The Unconscious Defectors, he called them.'

'That's all he ever speaks about.' Bridget hit back. 'That shrapnel he got in the kisser must have affected his brain as well.'

Nellie paused for thought before replying: 'Aye, you're right there Bridget … and it didn't do much for his looks, either. Did it?'

The laughter began in earnest and released the strain like the air from a punctured bike tyre as Bridget picked up the baton. 'But somebody once told me he was called Ugly Boab even before he was wounded. In fact, was he not Christened Ugly Boab?'

'Stop it Bridget. That's a shame. He can't help the way he looks.'

'It's a shame, all right. A shame for us. We've got to look at his horrible mug every time we go into his manky shop.'

There was a temporary pause as both women considered that salient observation before Bridget added: 'Think of his poor wife; having to sleep with him every night. Can you imagine it? Him snuggling up to her with his big, fat lips dripping with saliva. "Give's a kiss, Bunty? I'll make you happy".'

'He's like Boris Karloff on the prowl,' Nellie chimed up.

They allowed the sniggers to subside before Bridget set the ball rolling again. 'Mind you, Bunty's not a wee bit unlike Boris Karloff herself.'

The women stopped their double act to gather their thoughts and drink their sherry. Bridget's voice was faint and thin. 'Shooting deserters. Huh! Who the hell does he think he is? Ugly Boab just lost a customer.'

A look at the clock on the mantelpiece made her feel sick in her stomach. She knew that if Frank didn't come through the door within the next few minutes, he wouldn't be coming at all. *That bastard is supposed to be here to see John. He promised.* She still didn't know what excuse she'd give him for John's absence, though, if he were to arrive. A bridge still to cross. Maybe. *Please, don't let him come home.*

The years they'd had together before war summoned him had been hard, too often unpleasant; certainly passionless. There had been no future for them. She knew that, even if he didn't. John, and only John, kept them together.

Across the small table sat a wise, intermittently infuriating woman who thrived on tittle-tattle and scandal, but there was no doubting that Nellie had a kind heart. It was time for Bridget to give her neighbour what she craved, the story of Frank McGarrity and the visitors everybody seemed to know something about.

17

Frank and Leitch had come as close as was possible to begin to like each other. They reminisced about Dunkirk and the poor sods they had saved. There were recollections of the dramatic scenes of the evacuation of 350,000 Allied soldiers from the beaches of northern France a little more than a year earlier. How they dragged the wounded to safety and cradled men having breakdowns believing they were done for. They comforted dying soldiers, some with limbs blown off and lying nearby, in unimaginable pain, screaming and begging God to take them. No time to think. No seconds or minutes to dwell on the horror unfolding in front of them. No room for self-pity.

'We're just the same, you and me,' Leitch told him. 'Comrades.' He pointed at the three stripes on his arm. 'This doesn't make us any different. Do you think I asked for these? Somebody's got to be in charge, to accept responsibility. Would you? I doubt it, because you set yourself up as complainer-in-chief. Mr popular among the lads, like Stephen. Young, impressionable, easily led. Wouldn't it be better to set these kids an example?' Leitch probed and prodded his prisoner, hopeful there was some good in the man.

Frank's silent burp into a clenched fist preceded a slight moment of reflection as he considered his retort. 'Okay. I know I'm always ready with an opinion, or a joke,' he admitted, 'but maybe that's all about disguising my fear. That's what it is. There; I've confessed. I'm fucking scared. You know, I was shiting myself in France, wondering when the bullet was going to come. They said after 1918 that there'd never be another war. We believed them. Suddenly, we're dodging death in far-off lands. Families and friends left behind to worry.'

It was the first serious conversation in which he and Leitch, or Bert as he was now calling him, had engaged, aided by too many beers and the resultant slackening of tongues. There was an agreement that life in the Pioneer Corps called all too frequently for courage.

There was also a difference between being brave and what Leitch described as a 'toughness of character'.

'Courage could be driven by fear,' he contended. 'Being tough means being able to handle responsibility. It means you can cope with looking after others and not be self-obsessed. You can work alongside them. Gain their respect. Help them with their problems. That's being tough. What about you? Are you tough?'

It was a bit of an uncomfortable question for Frank as Leitch kept the heat on and reminded him a command had to be carried out to return to base with the errant soldier in tow or he would be in big trouble. He didn't want any problems to be tossed his way. It was a stern warning to McGarrity while, at the same time, trying to keep him onside.

'Toughness isn't just about how many drunks you can knock-out,' he told Frank, 'or how many Germans you can kill. If you think you're tough, try doing my job. You can't be liked all the time. And look around you. These lads might listen to your stories, laugh at your jokes, but do they like you? Do you have their respect?'

Was this too near the bone for McGarrity?

Stephen suddenly burst back into life and felt well enough to request another pint. There was a half-pint coming his way, Millie told him, purchased as he slumbered, by Frank, who signalled to the landlady that she should avoid giving him the whisky. Frank whispered that he would have it instead.

Cosgrove told himself 'you're fine now'. His body, as he was soon to discover, would have other ideas.

As the drinkers mingled, argued, chatted, smoked and joked, Leitch sidled over to Neep, for whom he felt some sympathy at being the butt of McGarrity's incessant jibes and japes. He understood the former footballer's awkwardness and his inability to laugh at himself, traits that were fuel for the pub's returned court jester. Neep and his nemesis were different sides of the same coin, he thought, each trying to be accepted in their own way, yet finding themselves on the outside, not that Frank would have agreed with that summation.

'I assume,' Neep said quietly, 'that he's done a runner. That's why you're here; to collect the deserter. What'll happen to him?'

Leitch was noncommittal. Neep had hoped to hear that McGarrity would be thrown in prison or, better still, placed in front of a firing squad, but as the sergeant shrugged his shoulders, he was left to wonder.

'Well, I hope they throw the book at the bastard,' Neep spat. 'I've no time for him and his obsession with what he sees as discrimination against his lot. It's all nonsense. What he doesn't know, because it's nobody's business, is that I'm from a mixed marriage. My mother was a Catholic, but she wasn't so hung up on it that she'd have walked away from the man she fell in love with. Her family weren't devout; nowhere near it. They were against separate communities. Aye, and separate schools. Breeds discontent, if you ask me. And, by the way, the Catholics aren't the only ones to be exploited by the mill owners. Just ask the workers at the other hell holes in Dundee, run by the Baxters and the Cairds and the Grimonds, and all the other jute barons. Ask *their* workforces if they're happy. Funny, we never hear about them from Archbishop McGarrity.'

Leitch nodded his head. He was intrigued by the divide and failed to see the ecclesiastical sense in it.

In his home town of Bradford, the partition was between the haves and the have nots. The have nots should all be on the same side. Religion played no part in the divisions in communities. To him, it all sounded so negative, so pointless. Surely, poverty and its causes were the common enemy.

'Of course it's negative,' Neep agreed, 'but nobody has the answer. It just rumbles on and on, and even though things might change after the war, the bile between two faiths, both Christian, will still be with us.'

Bert was grateful that there was someone sane among the Nine Bells' eccentric patrons. Or, should that be patients? He wondered about the mental health of a few of them.

Back in their world, the general discussion turned once more to the day's main talking point - the Harp and the Violet - as Frank revealed that it was one of Gino's countrymen who had scored the winner for the team in green.

'Sid Paccione was the hero,' he said. 'And, by the way, he scored the goal with his head, just to prove that Neep hasn't got exclusive rights on useful bonces.'

The former Violet centre-forward blew air from puffed-up cheeks and looked at Leitch as if to say 'I told you. He can't help it, mocking others.' The sergeant smiled knowingly as Frank's put-down underlined that he was usually on the front foot when it came to humiliation.

Millie spotted the signals. Quarrelling had to be met with force and halted at source. 'Change the subject,' she hollered. Her preference was to hear from the lads from England, which is why she threw-in her own tuppence-worth. 'You boys will be missing your families, eh?'

Stephen began to slur and slobber his way through a story that within a few seconds brought an eerie silence to those in his immediate vicinity. It cut right through the fumes from the Woodbine and the roll-ups, smoke dancing across wrinkled faces, while Neep's pipe created a cloudscape above the heads of the drinkers.

'Family? The youngest person in the pub looked downwards for a moment, then spoke softly, slowly picking through every word as he tried to move his foggy brain into gear. 'No family to miss.' Those few simple words prompted looks of anticipation among the punters. It was a preamble that almost forced them to listen to the story about to be imparted.

'Did you read about the Woolwich bombing last year? At Woolworths?' He did not wait for anyone to answer. 'My mother and father were both killed in that. Last November. Six months ago. Hm! Seems like yesterday.'

The hush that descended on the room was as solid as concrete as Cosgrove continued. 'One minute they were happy together. They did everything together. The next, they were dead; together.'

He stared ahead as he continued. 'Saturday shoppers. Snuffed out. A hundred and sixty-eight innocent people. Dead. Or dying.'

There was an intensity cloaking the listeners who felt Stephen's pain. Heads drooped. They might have thought how lucky they were that they were still breathing in the midst of such butchery across Britain and Europe.

Only Millie spoke. She cleared her throat and patted the young soldier's hand, still within lifting distance of his drink on the bar. 'Sorry to hear that, son. The war's been hell. More hell for some than for others. Sometimes I curse my luck at being alive at this time in our history. I mean, what have we done to deserve this? I know people will say we can't think like that. If we did, Hitler would be here, they say. We'd be German slaves, and all that. I've read about what they've done to places all over the country. Look what happened a few weeks ago in Glasgow. Six hundred and fifty dead over two nights of bombing. Clydebank, too. And all those poor souls in Coventry. Aye, the Luftwaffe has been busy across our skies.'

Millie recounted stories of other bombings and lives claimed and recalled how, also the previous November, eight bombs were dropped on Dundee, one terrifyingly close to a packed cinema in Forest Park. The raids had been aimed at the destruction of the Tay Bridge but as the RAF chased off the enemy planes, the German pilots unloaded their bombs to allow them to escape more speedily. Several innocent Dundonians were collateral damage.

She held the floor. 'I know somebody who knows a man and his wife who went to the pictures that night and they took a couple of kids from up their close with them. They heard three or four loud bangs. They thought it was some young rascals trying to kick-in the double doors leading to Forest Park Road.

'They said that the lights went out and somebody screamed. Then, a man stood on a seat and called for everybody not to panic. The manager went on the stage and calmed everybody before the emergency generator became operational and he asked the people if they wanted to see the rest of the film. Of course they did. They'd paid good money, four pence for the adults and tuppence for the children.'

In Dundee, the price of things, even the cheap seats at Forest Park picture house, was important information in any conversation.

'So, the film went on,' Millie added, 'but a quarter of an hour later the usherette came in with her torch and led everybody out. They didn't know why, but when they reached the street everything was in darkness and there was debris all over the place; bricks, stones, glass. Even chimneys. Shop windows were blown in, as well.

'The bombs that fell out of the sky that night landed only twenty yards from the pictures. Can you imagine the scale of the deaths and injuries if it had hit the cinema?'

Frank joined in. He was sympathetic as he tried to steer Cosgrove's thoughts away from the memory of the deaths of his parents.

'Coventry,' he said. 'We were there. You remember that, Stephen? Clearing up the mess? That's what we do. Buildings flattened, people buried.'

The silence was awkward as Frank did his best to nudge the youngster out of his melancholy. 'And then, you look at what we've done. The British. We've bombed German civilians, too.'

'The bastards started it,' Neep hissed from his table.

'Yeah.' Stephen suddenly snapped out of his dwam. He turned to Frank and nodded. 'And what about when we were in Dunkirk last year and the people who lived there. No food, no milk, hardly any meat. Starving. They were eating the horses killed by the bombs.' He shook his head despairingly, sighed loudly and swallowed hard. 'Horses! Can you believe it?'

A veil of silence fell on the gathering, broken only by another of Gino's homilies. 'Horses? They're-a eating horses *here*. Listen lads. You as well Millie. Did to hear aboot-a Dan Murray, the butcher? Him at the Sosh doon the road? *He* sells horse meat a' the time. Puts it in-a the mincer and the women, they cannae tell-a the difference. They're in the next week and they're-a saying: "Oh Dan, that was-a lovely mince I got last week. Do you think you can-a manage a wee quarter pound for-a my man's tea the night?" The daft buggers. They're-a eating deid horses. Murray; he sends that lad Charlie Cooper doon to that shop at the bottom o' the Wellgate to collect-a the horse meat. In a suitcase. As if he's goin' on-a his holidays. I'm-a tellin' you, they're crazy, the twa o' them.'

108

There was an all-round appreciation of Gino's narrative, not to say a smattering of disbelief. They didn't care. The Campania comedian's timing was always perfect. He knew when to pause to allow space for the laughs, and his broken English made his performance all the more riveting. There was more to tell about Dan Murray, the demon butcher.

'He's gonna get-a caught one-a these days,' was Gino's determination. The shrunken, olive skinned man from the toe of Italy seemed to have grown a few inches by virtue of being the centre of attention and able to generate some laughs.

He felt sure phase two of his anecdote would be another winner. He invited them to prick up their ears, flicking his fingers towards his body to pull them in and in seconds, he had their full attention as they edged closer to him. Neep, Gerald and Norman listened from the fringes, none wishing to miss a single syllable.

'Dan, he gets-a the message at the shop fae a man in the toon.' Gino began. 'A baker. "I'm-a desperate," says the man. "I need-a your help." So, the bold Murray, he sees a chance to mak-a some extra cash on the side. He asks the baker what is-a the matter? The baker, he tells him he's-a catering for a weddin'. Posh people. They want-a steak-a pies. Steak-a pies! Has he no' heard aboot-a the rationing? He canna get-a meat onywhere, says the baker. He offers good money if Dan can get-a the beef. So Murray, he says: "Leave it-a wi' me. I get-a you beef in twa or three days".'

Gino paused as he waited for that part of his yarn to filter through to the assemblage. He swallowed his beer and looked at the open-jawed listeners, some of whom began to think his story had ended on an anticlimactic note.

'Was that it?' Millie was impatient. 'Did he get the bloody beef? Are you gonna tell us, or what? Or are we supposed to guess?'

Gino placed his beer on the bar and raised two open hands, the palms facing his questioner. 'Forbearance, Millie,' he begged. 'Murray; he's-a trying a' ower the toon for-a the beef. Ony beef. He cannae get it. Nae beef. Nae horse meat. No' even the condemned-a beef he sometimes sells, that naebody kens aboot. But-a the deal, it wisnae aff. No. Murray, he try one-a last contact. The man at-a the slaughterhoose doon at Dock Street. The man tells him: "I'm-a sorry, Dan. I cannae help. It's no' possible. I'm a' oot o' the beef." Then the man thinks for a wee bit, and he says: "The only thing I have is a 37-year-old deid donkey".

"I'll tak it," says-a Murray, quick as a flash.'

'You're joking.' Millie's eyes widened. She was incredulous. Her mouth fell open. 'A donkey? You're saying he bought a donkey?'

Gino opened his arms, his mouth down at the corners. He nodded: 'Thirty-seven ... auld ... frail ... skinny ... deid.'

'Wait. You're not telling us he took it.' Millie was hooked, positively aching to hear the next instalment of the saga.

'Of course-a he took it,' Gino stated matter-of-factly. 'It was-a needed. He didnae want to spoil-a the poor lassie's big day. So, he gets into the Sosh after-a closing time on Thursday night. He butchers the donkey in-a the back shop, minces it and-a he cooks it a' through the night for-a the steak-a pies for-a the wedding. It was a' done and aff to the bakers for the pastry, lang afore-a the shop opened the next-a mornin'.'

Millie was so captivated she hadn't wiped the bar for several minutes. 'So, you're saying the baker never knew what was in the pies?'

'Are you-a daft?' Gino continued. 'Of course-a he disnae ken. How would he ken? He disna want to ken. He's-a happy. He gets-a his steak-a pies, though technically they're no' really steak. The weddin' goes on and he and-a Murray are quid's-in.'

'So, in the end, everybody's happy, eh?' Millie re-started her bar dighting.

'Of course a'body's happy.' Gino took another sip of his drink. 'Well, a'body except the thirteen guests wha' were rushed tae the hospital wi' the food-a poisoning. A'body else, they were-a fine. They just-a blame it on-a the bug that's-a goin' aroond. Naebody kens ony different.'

Tears of laughter flowed from Leitch's eyes. He shook his head in wonder and elbowed Cosgrove. 'What did I tell you?' he purred. 'We're in the land of nutters here.'

But Stephen's stupefied mind had already wandered at some point during Gino's party piece. His thirst, but only for Scottish beer of the McEwan's pale ale variety, could not be slaked. 'Another drink, Molly,' he demanded.

'The name's Millie.' Her curt response and the timbre of her voice, more bass baritone than mezzo soprano, demanded that: 'You can call me Mrs Barton. And take it easy, young man. My beer's stronger than that pish you're used to south of the border.'

18

The Bristol Cream had taken a bit of a hammering. It helped remove inhibitions and loosen tongues. More personal information sprinkled the conversation as Bridget and Nellie comforted each other and hoped for better days for themselves and the downtrodden women who, in wartime, battled each day against poverty, pitiful wages and repression.

Many were cowed by cowardly men, all too ready to browbeat and bully their spouses within the confines of their own homes, usually, but not exclusively, at the end of a night's drinking. Wife-beating was something of a cottage industry in parts of Tipperary and life in Lochee was always somebody's bad dream.

But there was a spirit of determination and stoicism among Dundee's women, keeping their families together while scrimping through life on meagre wages in return for their daily hell in the city's mills. It underscored a certain bond between them; more sisters of misery than sisters of mercy.

Many of those women had had trouble resigning themselves to the unpalatable story, still fresh in their minds, that while their men were at war, mainly with the Black Watch, the traditional regiment of Tayside, people like Jessie Jordan, who ran a hairdressing salon off Dundee's Hilltown, had been doing their best to scupper the war effort, at least in Britain. Jordan was caught just before the outbreak of hostilities spying for the enemy and thrown into Saughton prison in Edinburgh, then moved to Craiginches jail in Aberdeen.

The Glasgow-born hairdresser, who had returned to Scotland after twenty-five years of living in Deutschland following her marriage to a German in 1921, allowed her premises to be used as a 'post-box' where mail was sent before being forwarded to other agents of the Abwehr, the Fatherland's military intelligence.

'She's two years into her four-year sentence,' said Nellie, 'and now they're talking about releasing her and putting her in an internment camp. Jesus God! What's the world coming to? I'd have locked the bugger up and thrown away the key.'

Bridget did not disagree. She had her own anecdote about the secret agent. 'There's a tenter works beside me. His sister went to Jordan's shop to get her haircut once. Wanted a new style. Shorter; like Claudette Colbert.'

'Oh, I liked her in that film Zaza, with Herbert Marshall. Saw it at the Rialto. Or was it the Astoria? Can't remember. Me and my sister Ruby.' Nellie was off once more on another path.

'Anyway,' Bridget frowned as she continued her spiel, 'the tenter's sister says Jordan could hardly speak English. Apparently, she'd had a hairdressing business in Hamburg. Hamburg! Imagine that. And she'd been married twice to Huns, by the way.'

'Aye. She was caught bonnie, that Jordan.' Nellie piped-up. 'That woman that worked for her; Mary Curran, went into her bag and found a map of Scotland's barracks and all those coastal defence bases. Rosyth, and all those places. I'd have cut her hand off.'

'Aye, that wouldn't have been an unfair punishment for Jordan.'

'Naw! Not Jordan. That Curran woman. Imagine going into somebody's handbag.'

The outbreak of laughter was spontaneous. They shrilled like two schoolgirls discussing boys on whom they had a crush and, at that moment, had simultaneously entered the same comfort zone. They were at ease with each other and chuckled away to themselves as they progressed towards draining the sherry bottle and made 'ah!' sounds of satisfaction as each drop caressed their tonsils.

'He's so good looking. Has a wooden leg, you know.' Bridget looked bewildered as Nellie broke the silence.

'Who's got a wooden leg? What are you talking about, Nellie?'

'Herbert Marshall. Lost it in the first war. You can't tell, mind. Well, not till he takes off his clothes, I suppose, although you never see him with his clothes off in the films, right enough. That's probably why. The leg.'

Nellie had momentarily stepped into her own world before returning to the subject of the secret agent crimper. 'Aye, that Mary Curran tipped-off the polis and then MI5 got involved. I read all about the trial. Every word. It was a good job Jordan co-operated. That's the reason the bugger only got four years.'

'You're not wrong there, Nellie,' Bridget nodded as her guest helped herself to another glass of sherry. 'But I mean, what kind of country recruits a hairdresser as a spy? Especially one that's not very good. At cutting hair, that is. Or spying, come to think of it. Otherwise she wouldn't have got caught. By the way, the tenter says his sister looked nothing like Claudette Colbert when Jordan had finished with her. More like Herbert Marshall.' Cue more giggling.

The quiet moments that followed produced a change in Nellie's mood, from merry to maudlin, aided by the sherry. Soon, she was showing signs of raw emotion. She confessed she still missed her husband Jack, killed on day one of the Battle of Loos in 1915.

'I think about him every single day,' she said. 'He joined up as soon as he could. He was about the age your Frank is now. Never selfish.' She held back in contemplation and lowered her head, and a sad smile appeared on her wrinkled face. 'Except once; when he went and got himself killed and left me behind.'

The tears welled-up in the eyes of the woman who found herself in Tipperary as a toddler, one of many who had trudged from Glasgow, holding the hands of their mothers all the way. They would set up a makeshift tent each night just off the deserted roads and harboured hopes of a lift from a friendly lorry driver in the mornings.

'Daft, isn't it?' she went on, wiping her eyes with a small handkerchief she conjured from inside the sleeve of her moth-eaten cardigan. 'Nearly twenty-six years he's been gone.' She looked to the side, to nothing in particular.

Her voice was feeble and barely audible as she sniffed her way through what was troubling her. 'I mind the first time I saw him. He and his brother had the firewood business and they were going around the doors selling kindling. He knocked on our door and I answered it. My mother was shouting in her broad Glasgow accent: "Whaw is it?" I couldn't speak for staring at him. Tall, slim, straight-backed. And that moustache. God, he was proud of that moustache. He was so handsome. My mother said I was dribbling at the mouth for an hour and a half after he left. We never bought any kindling.'

Bridget felt for her old neighbour, childless and lonely, but always ready to help when it was needed, even though her nosiness was sometimes irksome. She looked-out for John when some of the bigger boys would start their bullying. She would clip them round the ears and shoosh them away with a 'get your arses out o' here you little buggers or I'll be up at your door to speak to your mothers.'

'Everybody said he was a fine big man, your Jack. Always kind to bairns.' Bridget knew how important such reminiscences were to Nellie, especially if they could be shared with a friendly face.

'Aye, that he was. A true gentleman. I just wish we'd been able to have … well, it doesn't matter now.'

'Did you ever think about marrying again? You were just young when Jack … you know.'

'Hah! Who'd have a widow like me; smelling of the mill? My man's family had a bit of money in years to come, because of the firewood business and the coal deliveries that came later. A couple of lorries; the depot. Aye, plenty money, but I never saw any of it. Jack went off to France and his brother was left to look after things. He was supposed to see I was taken care of, but the emphasis was on the mother and the sisters. I was soon dumped when Jack was killed. September 25, 1915. I'll never forget that date.'

Bridget felt Nellie's distress as the memories flooded every nook and cranny of her mind. She squeezed her hand across the table and poured herself the last of the sherry as if to signal it was time to change the subject. It was always better with some cheeriness in the air, she reckoned.

'I see they're saying Russia might soon be in the war.' Bridget clutched at straws for a new topic of conversation, to steer it away from Jack – and Herbert Marshall's solitary leg. 'And I read in the Courier that the wife of the American ambassador said her man's been egging her on to practice falling flat when she hears the air raid sirens. Imagine.'

It was inconsequential chatter, but it sparked Nellie back to life as she commented: 'She just needs to get herself down to Millie Barton's to learn that. They're falling flat on their faces there every Saturday night.'

It was a remark that automatically brought the discussion back to where it had begun, to Frank.

Nellie toyed with her now empty sherry glass and admitted she worried about Bridget and John and what kind of future they had with a man she deemed wholly unsuitable as husband and father material.

'I don't like to see Frank walk all over you,' she said. 'I mean, let's face it, you've been carrying the family all these years, long before he went off to the war. It's been a heavy load for you. You're bound to feel it.'

Bridget conceded that point, but she had always held on to the hope that he would change, improve, evolve. His brief excursion back to Lochee, however, did not fill her with even a scintilla of positivity on that score. The aspirations for better accommodation with a garden, a bathroom, a separate bedroom for John had ebbed away over the years as she watched her ambivalent, rudderless husband tread water with his life.

Sure, he had made promises. His words often filled her with hope. Only the previous night he attempted to make her believe that a job and a new council house would be theirs at the cessation of hostilities. Deep down, though, she didn't have faith in those assurances. The needle had stuck. He was shallow and selfish. She learned that early on in their time together. There were psychopathic characteristics, too, that were ingrained in his psyche; and indifference to her and John, superficial charm, no discernable conscience. If confirmation of those traits were needed, it came when he took off to the pub and the Harp and Violet football match with the soldiers, relieving her of the coins from her biscuit-tin bank; a pittance of pennies for a rainy day and an occasional treat for John.

What kind of man does that, hours after his return following two years apart from his family?

She could not erase that thought from her mind. This time, though, it was different. Because Bridget didn't care.

Nellie shuffled nervously in her chair. Her young host began to notice a twitchiness about her guest as she cleared her throat a couple of times and uttered idle, meaningless, unfinished remarks. 'Aye, well ...' and 'Nobody knows what the future holds ...' and 'The good Lord will sort things out ...'

This quiet reflection, with each woman grappling with their own thoughts, was snapped as the matter that had niggled Nellie for some time was brought out for an airing. She could contain herself no longer and, despite her uncertainty over the wisdom of whether to utter the words that were on the tip of her tongue, she was ready to throw caution to the wind.

Should she ask her question? How would Bridget react? Would she consider it the height of impertinence? Nellie did not like some of the answers she heard inside her own head. There was still a reticence, however slight, to take the plunge. Nonetheless, she inhaled noisily then blurted it out. 'That handsome young man who's been coming by, Bridget; is he somebody special?'

Like a boxer under attack and attempting to dodge an opponent's punches, Bridget bobbed and weaved and had to think on her feet.

Should I be truthful about Harry? Or maybe I can make up some reason for his visits? Don't be stupid. Why would he be calling round here, week-in, week-out? I could always just brazen it out.

She had a speedy decision to make, but, in the end, knew she could not hide from the truth. 'He's a friend, Nellie; a good friend, who's looking out for me. He's single, and we enjoy each other's company. And that's really all there is to it.'

This did not satisfy the neighbour with eyes and ears everywhere. It was too bland, as if Bridget had brushed the inquiry away with the swish of a hand. Not enough detail. More importantly, it gave no hint of the romance Nellie suspected, or of its strength. Bridget knew the inquisition was just beginning. Jessie Jordan, she suspected, would have had a tough time explaining her extra-curricular activities had Nellie been at the other side of the desk as the arresting officer at Bell Street police station.

117

'You like him, then?' Counsel for the prosecution continued. Bridget was aware that, in her old friend's world 'like' meant 'love', a word rarely breathed in Lochee, or other working-class areas for that matter. It was foreign, too, to most men, until they needed their wives to part with a couple of bob for the pub. Harry, however, did not shy away from using it, as Bridget could attest.

'Yes. I like him. He's kind, gentle, thoughtful and clever; all the things Frank isn't.'

'So, where do you see yourself and your thoughtful friend going from here?'

Bridget smiled and shook her head. 'That's all you're going to get out of me, Nellie Gribben.'

19

A raucous Saturday night in the Nine Bells would be nothing without a sing-song. At least that's what Frank always believed when he was in the place, especially if he was the one who wanted to sing, which was usually the case. He believed he was a more than competent crooner.

It may have been a couple of years since he had taken his leave of Lochee, but he saw no reason not to pick up where he had left off. After all, he was suitably lubricated and needed no encouragement, save for that provided by the beers and the whiskies he had consumed. He was ready and itching to do his turn as soon as Gerald Murphy had finished his rendition of *Danny Boy*.

Frank's experience of Murphy's past musical exploits were that he had trouble finding the right key, fumbled for the correct notes, elasticised them until he hit them, and frequently forgot the lyrics of whatever dirge he chose to share with an audience that didn't listen. This meant a song that would normally last three minutes, would be significantly longer. Gerald's first lines were a reminder that he was not cut out for the stage.

'Oh Danny Booooyyyy
The pipes, the pipes are callinnng
From glen to glennnnn, and down the mountainside
He would also take infrequent sips of his beer during the course of his rendition thus extending the song even more. Much too long for Frank's liking. The caustic comments he made as Lochee's frustrated Count John McCormack sang his heart out, underscored McGarrity's impatience. McCormack's most memorable song - *It's a Long Way to Tipperary* - resonated with the people of Lochee, despite it being about the *real* Tipperary, although those who lived in the one close by would have expressed their delight that the celebrated Irish tenor was conferred a Papal Count by Pope Pius XI in recognition of his work for Catholic charities.

'Get a move on, Gerry, I've got a train to catch' and 'Danny Boy'll be a man by the time you've finished.' Frank sneered, impatient to perform *The Wild Colonial Boy,* which topped his musical repertoire. No sooner had the ripple of applause for the previous singer subsided, than he launched into the ballad.

Neep, caught too close to the singing soldier as he arrived at the counter for another beer, was not impressed with the impromptu cabaret. Why would he be? He despised McGarrity with a vengeance. That much, everybody knew.

'Listen to him,' he said to Leitch. 'What did I tell you? He's besotted with Ireland and the Irish. He wants to be Irish. If he loves the place that much he should emigrate there. I'd gladly pay his boat fare.'

An eavesdropping Gino sprang to Frank's defence. 'But it's a good-a song wi' a good-a story. And the Wild-a Colonial Boy, he's-a like me - an immigrant. He went to Australia. And I came to Lochee. Look at-a Frank. He thinks he's-a the laddie in the song.'

By the final verse, the customers' full attention was on the singer:

He fired a shot at Kelly, which brought him to the ground
And turning round to Davis, he received a mortal wound
A bullet pierced his proud young heart, from the pistol of Fitzroy
And that was how they captured him, the Wild Colonial Boy.

'Another one of your talents, eh?' Cosgrove's slurred sarcasm was heard, but ignored. It didn't stop the impudent serviceman. 'Singer, comedian, storyteller. Bullshitter.'

But Frank would not be wrong-footed by his drunken friend's disparagement. He judged the barbs insignificant and unimportant, the rant of a kid who could not hold his bevvy. He issued a light-hearted warning to Leitch that the youngest member of their travelling party would have to be watched. 'Keep an eye on him, Bert. He's getting a wee bit cocky. The jungle juice up here is too much for that wee laddie.'

Stephen's mood had notably altered over the previous hour or so. He was morose, downbeat and disgruntled, no longer disposed to being a target for ridicule. 'Here we go. Use your usual method to get attention; mockery and sarcasm. But you'll never put me down.'

Frank sought to make comedic collateral from the situation. He placed an arm around his colleague and told him he would never try to put him down. He was merely concerned for his wellbeing, especially as he had swallowed too much strong Scottish beer 'for your underdeveloped little body'.

This new tension in the air was unmistakable, uncomfortable for the others.

The friction between the idol and his principal admirer was there for all to see and when Stephen pushed Frank's arm away and muttered that 'one of these days McGarrity, I'll ...' his compatriot cut him off, leaned-in and whispered: 'Whatever it is you have in mind son, it'll not be happening today.'

Once more Gino entered the fray from stage left to try and deactivate a potential explosive scenario and, unusually for him, ordered up drinks for the visitors before turning to Frank with a leading question the Nine Bells' clientele wanted answered. 'So, tell us-a the story. Is it-a true that you buggered-aff fae the army? Because, you canna just a run awa'. No' when we're at-a war.'

Frank rattled off two or three reasons for his unscheduled, if temporary, departure from armed service; he was confused and depressed, he said. He felt he was in a hopeless situation. How could those in the bar, aside from Leitch and Cosgrove, possibly understand what went on in the mind of someone who had witnessed the horrors of war? It was a sound and reasoned argument.

However, the peace that had fallen like a veil on the room lasted no more than thirty seconds. Neep, unsympathetic and still stewing with anger and hatred from his earlier contretemps with the man he disliked most in Lochee and probably beyond, lobbed in a hand grenade of an observation along the lines that McGarrity was seeking excuses for what was nothing more than bare-faced cowardice.

Looks flew between Hughie and Millie, each fearing a battle of cowboy movie proportions was about to erupt where the saloon is wrecked as fists fly and the bar tender is lifted by a hulking brute and tossed against the big mirror behind the bar. Hughie did not like that idea. Millie would have needed more than one man to raise her off the ground, on the other hand. She would be safe in a bar-room brawl, mainly because of the threat of a life ban from her beloved establishment.

Hughie quivered and the sturdy landlady straightened her shoulders, pushed out her opera singer-sized chest and psyched herself up. Would she become a peacemaker or a dictator unwilling to take prisoners? The latter was the obvious outcome should the problem escalate. Lochee's Joan of Arc stood ready.

'Sounds like a cop-out, if you ask me.' Neep nonchalantly drank from his pint glass following his throwaway line from the side of his mouth. He was of no mind to keep a lid on his opinions. 'Depression? What does that mean? Let's face it; you're not the hard man you're always making out you are.'

Eyes turned towards Millie. Her bar polishing grew more frantic as the adrenaline pumped vigorously through her veins and the potential for fisticuffs edged closer to reality. A nervy Hughie was busy trying to look busy. When would Mrs Barton step-in? She's the boss, he thought. It was her responsibility. Not his. Hughie was a worrier, not a warrior.

'You know something,' Frank growled in Neep's direction, 'your mouth's as big as your head. If you were twenty years younger …'

Another bang on the bar as a prelude to Millie exerting her considerable authority. 'Enough! I'm not having this. Keep Neep's head out of this. That's personal. This is a pub where people come to enjoy a drink without getting into a fight.' She paused to allow time for Neep and Frank to digest her stern words. 'So, you either cut it out right now, or you're barred.'

The warning worked. The protagonists were suitably chastened. An atmosphere of relative tranquillity dropped in on proceedings as a fear of being ejected and suspended indefinitely by Lochee's toughest landlady hit hard. It was, though, a peace of the short-term variety, broken by a slobbering, unsteady Stephen.

'BIG. FUCKING. MOUTH.' Those three words drew eyes towards the young private. 'What?' he demanded of the men looking at him. 'What are you all staring at? Am I not allowed to say what's on my mind? Frank's got a big mouth. We all know that. Always spouting off about something. Usually just stating the obvious. Nobody's going to dispute that.'

His eyes rolled a little as he once more expelled the gas from Millie's beer into the smokey atmosphere. But he wasn't finished. The oration continued. 'Neep, you'll have heard all his boasts and bluster. You've probably committed them all to memory. And you, too, Gino. Christ knows, he's told anybody and everybody in our unit who'd listen. He's built-up this reputation, you know, about being a fighting man, a tough guy. Mind you, none of the lads in the regiment have actually seen him fighting. So, what can we deduce from this?' He looked around the room before adding, staccato-style: 'That ... he ... is ... full ...of ... shite.'

Frank's self-professed reputation was suddenly at stake. He was seething as he took Stephen back a few hours in time, to the height of Lochee's principal sporting event, the Harp versus the Violet. He reminded him how, had he not been held back by his companions, he would have choked the opposition supporter he'd encountered 'with the bastard's own dark blue and white scarf'.

Stephen sneered and poo-pooed the claim with a shake of the head. Frank, he swore, had made a show of preparing to attack the Violet fan, but knew, particularly as he was a prisoner, that his guards would not allow him to aggravate an already tricky state of affairs.

This triggered more vitriol from the McGarrity vocabulary. Millie sucked air through clenched teeth. She gave each of them 'the look' which said: *'Keep this up and you will never set foot in my pub again.'* Not that this was ever likely.

Gino, who always seemed to have a story up his sleeve, took over. He was the kind of man needed in such circumstances to deactivate the bomb. 'Hey, Neep,' he called out to the surly solo drinker, quietly sousing himself in the corner. 'You still fancy one o' the OK sisters?

Neep grunted and ignored Gino's rhetoric.

Still, it pricked the curiosity of Leitch, eager to turn the spotlight away from the argumentative members of his unit. 'The OK sisters?' he queried. To him, they sounded like a music hall act who sang and danced. Until all was explained.

'They're-a twa local beauties. Auld maids. Sisters.' Gino embarked on another journey into the forest of local folklore.

123

'And they are inseparable. They walk-a doon the street like-a this.' He enlisted the help of Frank as they linked arms to demonstrate. 'One-a wi' the bandy legs and the other wi' the one bent knee turned in towards her other leg. So, if you're-a walkin' towards them, the one on-a the left is bow-legged like-a the letter O and the other wi' the funny knee, her legs look like a K. The OK sisters. It's-a quite a sight.'

Leitch shook his head and laughed out loud as he pictured the scene before Gino announced: 'I could-a never understand why they dinna get-a that stuff for their legs. '

'What are you talking about?' Millie inquired. 'What stuff?'

'I saw it advertised in-a the paper,' Gino explained. 'Panacel Antiseptic Ointment. You just rub it on and it-a clears up the legs. My wife, she has it. For her-a comatose veins.'

Millie and Hughie looked at each other as if to say 'here we go again'. Leitch chuckled at Gino's latest malapropism. Then, without warning, the sergeant sank the dregs of his beer and announced that it was time to leave.

But Frank, now well-oiled and feeling content at being back in his own surroundings, even with the arguments and insults thrown-in for good measure, protested that there was still valuable drinking minutes to spare before saying his goodbyes to Bridget and John.

'I'm sorry,' said Leitch. 'Out of the question. We've spent far too long here. We must head right down to the railway station.' He ordered Stephen to finish his drink.

'But I haven't seen John ...' Frank pleaded.

'No time. We're in big trouble if we miss that train. You're already on borrowed time.'

Frank recognised his grave miscalculation, his blunder; his inability to act responsibly. 'Fuck! I've ballsed it up again. What'll Bridget think of me? And John. I've let him down.' Draining his glass, he turned to his fellow drinkers. 'Well, it's been great seeing you all again. Even you, Neep. Not sure when I'll be back.'

There was more than a touch of bitterness in Cosgrove's voice. 'Back?' he laughed. You'll be lucky.'

That latest interjection simply ramped-up an already acute tension between him and McGarrity that had been escalating as the day had progressed. The commitment, not to say his promise to his wife, had become unimportant and forgotten. It was like three prisoners who'd been paroled for a weekend they did not want to end. Leitch, however, was secretly concerned about the growing strain in the relationship between the private and the prisoner. He placed a hand on Frank's arm to halt a verbal reaction that might have provoked a scrap.

'Go easy,' he whispered. 'He's pissed.'

As Frank held the door open for their departure, Neep suddenly perked up. 'Oi, McGarrity. I meant to ask you; how did Violet's young centre-forward play today? What's his name? Lewis. Harry Lewis.'

'Him!' Frank scoffed as he fixed his eyes on Neep. 'He's worse than useless. Never got near scoring.'

'Well, some people seem to like him. He's been scoring a lot lately. So I'm told, anyway.'

The pub doors closed behind the threesome. Eyes fixed on Neep. No-one said a word, but they knew what was behind his cheap jibe. A knife to the heart of his enemy. Well, it would have been, had Frank been au fait with the gossip surrounding his wife.

'You!' Millie was angry as she pointed at the warmongering Violet supporter. 'You're an evil swine. Just as well he clearly doesn't know.'

'Ach, keep your hair on, woman,' he snapped back. 'I was just asking how my nephew played today.'

Gino almost choked on his pale ale. 'Your-a nephew? He's-a the one up to the jiggery-pokery wi' the McGarrity wife?'

Neep sat in silence and shuffled his cap nervously around his little table and peered into the bottom of his near-empty tumbler.

'He plays-a for-a the Violet?' Gino's jaw was still gaping; his disbelief levels off the scale. 'So, he's a Proddie and she's-a …'

The mood inside the Nine Bells changed in the blink of an eye. There were looks of shock from all corners of the bar and the focus was on Neep. Answers were required. This was big news and every syllable had to be heard. He drained his glass, slowly, keeping his audience in suspense. 'It's nobody's business.' He dropped his head.

'Aye, right,' Hughie interrupted. 'Try telling that to Frank.'

A short, sharp 'shoosh' from Millie halted her lieutenant in his tracks. She nodded to Neep for him to continue. She would not be fobbed-off.

20

Somewhere above the chimneys of Lochee's coal-fuelled fires, the sky was bright. For the moment, hundreds of black plumes told the story of heat being generated in small, musty rooms in preparation for later on when people would huddle around fireplaces and their burning coals. It might be early May, but when the warmth of the spring sun receded, the chill of east Scotland moved in.

Meanwhile, cardigan-wearing little girls giggled, skipped and played hopscotch while the evening was still acceptably balmy. Boys kicked a ball around the rugged ground where earlier sheets and shirts and underwear had been hung out to dry. Others assumed roles as cowboys and Indians, firing make-believe pistols and rifles at each other from behind dykes and other structures shielding them from imaginary bullets. 'Casting' decisions had been established before the pretend film started.

'I'm Billy the Kid.'

'No, I bags him. You were him yesterday.'

'OK, I'll be Wyatt Earp'.

Women assembled at the foot of stairs for their weekly whispers. There were characters to assassinate, gossip to impart, scurrilous stories to be exchanged.

This was their Saturday night entertainment as they waited and wondered if and when their men would return from war. For those whose husbands were not in one of His Majesty's armed services, it was a waiting game until the pubs closed and the smell of beery breath gave way to the growl of snoring and snorting throughout a deep slumber.

Bridget remained indoors, away from uncomfortable questions and catty comments. Her umpteenth look at the ticking clock on the mantelpiece confirmed what she had suspected, that Frank's return to the Pioneer Corps barracks was already underway. Another McGarrity pledge had been broken.

Thank God I didn't bring John home and tell him his dad was coming to see him. The disappointment would have crushed him.

She wished she'd had Harry by her side; to talk, to feel the comfort of his embrace, to hold his hand. To feel his warm lips on the nape of her neck.

If only we had known each other before I'd met Frank, before that stupid night that started this nightmare.

Bridget's sheltered upbringing as one of nine siblings in a family welded to the Catholic faith meant her childhood was one of entrenchment in regular Mass and the holy sacraments. The crucifix on the wall above her sideboard underlined how it was nigh impossible to make a clean break from her religious upbringing. It was always there, but now more in the background.

For children at Dundee's Catholic schools, growing up was almost as strict as any prison regime. There were the Monday morning interrogations by teachers to 'out' those who had not attended church the previous day. What Mass did you go to? Who said Mass? What colour were the vestments the priest wore? Three correct answers were necessary to escape the wrath of a fundamentalist teacher with a thirst for corporal punishment. Two might just be lucky guesses.

Those who did not confess on a Friday, a day earmarked as meat-free for Lochee's Tims, were viewed with disdain by teachers as were their feeble excuses for not receiving the Eucharist. Breaking your fast between tea-time on Saturday and Mass on Sunday, if you intended to receive communion, was not permitted either. That there was a lack of food to be put on the tables of the devout and non-devout alike, did not seem to enter into the equation for followers of the teaching of the Church of Rome.

The 'starve yourself' edict was frequently hammered home deep into young minds, in church and in the classroom.

Christ suffered on the cross for us. The least we can do before we accept his body is make ourselves ready to receive him by fasting overnight.

The rule might just as well have said: *There will be no cocoa and jeelie pieces before bedtime on a Saturday.*

The shame and embarrassment, then, when Bridget fell victim to Frank's sexual inducement at eighteen years of age as she discovered intercourse for the first time, was almost too much to bear for the Gallachers. A decade on, Elsie's support for her daughter was still unshakable and Jim's love for John was as unyielding as the loathing he felt for the man who took his lassie's virginity.

*

'Are you needing some company?' Nellie's voice startled a drawn-looking Bridget as she put her head round the door. She was already in the house and seated before her neighbour's invitation to enter was issued. 'I thought you might want somebody with you. I take it you haven't heard anything?'

Bridget knew that Nellie would have been a fixture behind her net curtains as she stood at the bunker to monitor the comings and goings at her neighbour's house. She would have been at bursting point with curiosity over whether Frank and his captors had called in and the unthinkable had occurred, that she had missed their return.

'Nothing, Nellie; I've heard nothing, and I don't expect to. To be honest, I couldn't care less.' Bridget spoke with certainty more than resignation or sadness, as if a burden had been lifted off her shoulders. She felt as if she had reached a point in her life from which there would be no turning back. 'People who know what Frank's like, what he's *really* like used to say to me "it's just the Irish in him". What a load of tripe. He bangs on about his connection to Ireland, what with his grandparents coming from Roscommon and us living in Tipperary. It all sounds kind of romantic. A wee bit of the Emerald Isle carved out of Lochee. Huh! The Cox family knew what they were doing when they built this ghetto. Promise the workers from Glasgow and from across the Irish Sea that there are good jobs here. Then they put us into these pathetic, tumble-down properties while they sit up in their mansions. And their wives with nothing to do all day because they have servants to cook and clean.' If there was any doubt over whether her statement was vinegary, she promptly cleared it up. 'If that sounds bitter, it's because I am. The unfairness, that's what gets me.'

Nellie nodded in all the right places in a display of empathy. There would be no disagreement from this battle-scarred woman. In her mind, she still felt those aching muscles from her childhood walk from Glasgow, the misery, the constant 'when will we be there?' question directed at her weary, bedraggled, downtrodden mother, whose hope ebbed away with each step.

'I'll bet she didn't bargain on being one of two thousand sorry souls crammed into just 250 Tipperary houses,' Bridget mused.

Nellie urged Bridget to catch a tram from the High Street to Dundee city centre and race to the railway station to say her goodbyes to Frank. There was just time, she told her, and, as sensitively as she could, that: 'You don't know what can happen, Bridget. We're at war and ... well, you know, anything can happen. Anything.'

The inference wasn't lost on Bridget. Yet, she would not be budged. She had no wish to see Frank off from the railway station. His lack of devotion to her and to their son was irrefutable. It was close to zero. His failure to reappear after the football match merely highlighted that. He was gone and there was more than a little indifference inside her that he had not felt a strong enough pull towards his immediate family for him to abandon the pub and his cohorts whose company he preferred at such an important and pivotal time.

Bridget's decision was unequivocal: the marriage, whatever happened, was over. There was also a burning in her mind that she could not erase: *What if he didn't return from the war? What if ...?* Was this some kind of subconscious wish?

Nellie's antenna was still on high alert, however. Her gut feeling, honed after years of listening to hearsay, muckraking and scandal surrounding Frank, was that there was still something her neighbour was concealing. What was it? Was there more to pour from Bridget's lips?

'All marriages go through tough times.' Nellie prodded further as she adopted a commiserative approach, like a counsellor or a psychiatrist. She reached across the table and squeezed her young friend's hand. 'We just stick in and get on with it. That's the way we get through it.'

But Bridget's romance with Harry Lewis had moved her away from accepting the line that tolerating her current state of affairs was her only option. She had known too many miserable women in bad marriages, trapped in relationships of physical and mental abuse and of being told their job was no more than raising their families, keeping house and looking after their husbands. And, if possible, to earn a living. Many of the men inhabited a world of alcohol, gambling, womanising, unemployment and debt.

'You know my circumstances, Nellie,' Bridget said emphatically. 'Harry is too important to me. I will never abandon him and throw-in my lot with Frank. I'm not going back to the bad times.'

'But you're married. And there's the church. You know. No divorce, and all that. Excommunication, Bridget.'

'To hell with the church Nellie. You can't do this; you can't do that. Thou shalt not think for yourself. You've committed a sin. You'll have to pay for it. So, you make a mistake and then it's purgatory on earth for you for the rest of your life. You grow up with all that stuff hanging over your head. What kind of church is so rigid, so inflexible? I'll tell you; one that feeds on guilt and fear.'

The tempo of Bridget's peroration increased. She was calm and in control, and articulated her argument well as the words tumbled out. 'I'll not allow the church to dictate how I live the rest of my life and I'll fight anybody and anything who tries to drive a wedge between me and Harry. He's everything I ever wanted, Nellie. You only get one life and we're going make the best of it.'

Somehow, Nellie felt it was her duty to defend Catholicism and its ten commandments, particularly number six: *Thou shalt not commit adultery.*

Divorce, she insisted, was impossible, out of the question. It just couldn't happen in the religion they followed. 'I know we don't always agree with some of the church's teachings, but we follow them nonetheless. That's what we've been brought up to do and if we make mistakes God will forgive us. And he'll forgive you. You can't go on with this relationship, Bridget. It isn't right, and when the war is over you and Frank will settle back into married life and everything will be fine. Times are hard for us all.'

'I'll never break-up with Harry.'

'But Bridget ...'

'Nellie, I'm pregnant.'

21

Tay Bridge railway station was deserted, save for a porter who fussed around, trying to appear busy. McGarrity, Cosgrove and Leitch, all looking the worse for wear, descended the long flight of stairs from the street-level concourse to the grimness of platform one.

Frank and the sergeant chatted and laughed and joked, the former wondering how one of his gaiters had managed to become dislodged and go missing, while Leitch's passion for enforcing rules and regulations seemed to have evaporated, or at least diluted. Stephen, feeling queasy, sulked on a bench and hoped his nausea would not lead to something worse. A glance at the station clock told Frank they had almost half an hour to kill before the arrival of the Aberdeen to King's Cross, London, train. It set in motion the notion that there was enough time to grab just one more drink.

The suggestion was not rejected out of hand by his superior, himself in the merriest of moods. Meanwhile, the voice from the bench garbled its disagreement about what was being mooted.

'Hey, mate.' Leitch shouted over to the porter. 'London train on time?'

'As far as I know,' the porter replied, checking his pocket watch. 'Mind you, nothing's certain these days. It might be on time ... then again ... I'll keep you posted if there are any changes.'

Stephen's muddled mind informed him that all was not well with his stomach. The brain-to-breadbasket message didn't take long to get through as the retching started. He lowered his head between his knees and waited, but nothing came, save bile. His compatriots joked about his condition and his inability to hold his drink. It merely accentuated the young private's increasingly sulphurous opinion of his one-time friend.

'He's going through a Calvary of suffering,' McGarrity told Leitch and guffawed before turning his attention to the youngster. 'Tell you what, you sit there and try and empty your guts, 'cause that'll make you feel better for the journey, and me and Bert will nip up to the Club Bar and have one for the road. Loads of time. So, don't be fretting.'

'I'm not sure.' Leitch was now in the grip of prevarication and hesitation without being totally discouraging. 'We'd never have enough time. Would we? What if the train comes early?'

Frank pressed his proposal. He squared his shoulders to Leitch's body and placed a hand high on each of the sergeant's arms and looked him in the eyes. 'Think about it, Bert. It can't leave before it's due to leave. Eight thirty-five. That's what you said.'

Leitch once more toyed with the potential mayhem of missing the train; that all three would end up in the glasshouse along with other army miscreants who had fallen foul of military regulations. It was an observation that led Frank into a tunnel of reality. 'An army prison? At least it'll keep me out of trouble for a while.' He removed his hands from Bert's person and looked away momentarily before turning back to him. 'What do you think they'll hit me with?'

Leitch gave a shrug of uncertainty. His view was that because McGarrity would be returned to the unit within three days, he would probably serve a month inside. Had he been AWOL for longer, he'd have been locked-up for six months. It was wartime, after all.

'I never thought I'd say this, but I'm glad you came for me,' Frank admitted. 'I don't know what the hell I was thinking about, believing I could get away with it. But I couldn't take anymore.'

Behind them, Cosgrove's efforts to disgorge whatever was in his belly – Bridget's spam sandwiches, perhaps, and certainly enough beer to sink most of the German fleet – continued, as did Frank's teasing. He peppered each quip with an off-putting and exaggerated laugh. 'Fancy a wee plate o' mince and tatties, big man? A couple of Dan Murray's donkey pies, maybe?' The barbs kept coming. 'By the way, when the volcano does erupt, watch that none of the lava goes on your uniform. I don't want to be sitting next to somebody on the train who's stinking of puke.'

134

Suddenly, Leitch said something unexpected, perhaps to prevent all-out war between Cosgrove and McGarrity, now a fractured friendship and beyond repair. 'All right. Let's have that final drink. After all, think about where we are. We're in Gethsemane. All three of us.'

'Gethsemane? What are you on about?' Frank was puzzled.

'The garden of Gethsemane. You know, just before the crucifixion.'

'Oh aye. I remember that from school.'

'Have you heard of Rudyard Kipling?'

'No. Who's he?'

'He wrote a poem called Gethsemane during the last war.'

'Good for him.' Frank displayed his ignorance. 'Poetry was never my strong point. Miss Sweeney made us read Oliver Twist and A Tale of Two Cities.

Leitch had entered a serious, thoughtful zone. He explained how, in the poem, Kipling discussed the mental hell experienced by World War I soldiers with the speaker in the poem a soldier stationed in Picardy in France, thinking about his inevitable death in battle.

'He's praying in the field about the end of his life.' the sergeant told Frank. 'It's just like Christ praying in the Garden of Gethsemane before he was arrested and died on the cross. That's why Kipling even refers to the Bible when he says the soldier prayed that his cup might pass. Like Jesus, the soldier was unable to pass his cup.'

'Pass his cup?'

'The "cup" Jesus spoke of was the suffering He knew He was about to endure. That was his destiny. The soldier in France accepts that he must die for his country just as Jesus died for us.'

Frank showed scant interest in Bert's piece of religious education.

Then, in the silence of the railway station, Leitch, slowly and quietly, almost into himself, recited Kipling's words:

'The officer sat on the chair,
The men lay on the grass,
And all the time we halted there

I prayed my cup might pass.

It didn't pass—it didn't pass-
It didn't pass from me.
I drank it when we met the gas
Beyond Gethsemane!'

'So, you see Frank, our crucifixion awaits us, but it'll come in the form of a bullet or a bomb.'

'You're a religious man, then, Bert? Church of England?' He playfully put his fist to his chin. 'Still a Proddie,'

The sergeant grinned, put a hand on his prisoner's shoulder and shook his head. 'Actually, I'm a Catholic.'

Frank could hardly compute what he had just heard. 'That'll be right. You, a Catholic? Just like me?'

'No, Frank nothing like you,' he answered. 'I've never felt the need to publicise my Catholic faith. I never saw the point.'

In the silent moments that followed as Frank tried to grasp the meaning of the last five words of Leitch's declaration, Stephen stirred from his bench, yellow bile dribbling from the side of his mouth.

The porter passed by and the sergeant asked: 'What was the score at Hampden today pal?' The question reminded Frank there had been another important football match that day.

'It was 3-1 to England.' In an instant, the porter was gone.

'Bastards! I said they'd get beat without any Celtic players in the team,' Frank blurted out. He looked at Leitch. 'Didn't I? I told them in the pub. You mind?'

'Too good for you, eh?' Cosgrove stammered almost unintelligibly. 'And on your own turf, too. Maybe that'll keep your big gob shut for a while.'

Frank looked to Leitch, by now feeling sluggish and subdued by the amount of alcohol he'd swallowed over the course of the day. He then pointed a lazy finger at Stephen. 'Christ. It comes to life.'

But his erstwhile admirer would not be silenced. 'When is it going to sink in, McGarrity? We're all fed up with your crap. Your arrogance. All talk, as usual. But you never seem to get the message that nobody really listens to you.'

'Well, the only thing I can say to that,' Frank responded, 'is that you're coming dangerously close to a real smack in the mouth.'

The tit for tat became too much for the sergeant. 'Will you two stop bickering,' he demanded. 'You're giving me 'eadache.' His raised voice had no impact.

'Aye,' said Frank, 'and he's a pain in the arse. I hate these guys who suddenly become brave when they've had a few pints.' He rifled through his pockets and pulled out a two shilling coin. 'What've you got?' Leitch matched it. Enough for a couple of pints.

'Listen, Bert.' Frank looked and sounded stern, as if he had something important to say. 'I'm going to jail and you'll be off to some God forsaken hole to carry the wounded or be up to your bollocks in death. You'll never see the inside of a pub for months, years maybe. So, let's make the best of what time we've got left.

'I'll go on my own, if you don't want to come. I could murder another pint. A final pint. I'll be back in plenty of time for the train. I promise. You're a good lad. A comrade, eh? You said it. And a Tim. Who'd have thought? I'd never land you in it. Here's my hand on it.'

As they shook hands on the vow, Cosgrove began to feel hot and sweaty as he fumbled at the side of his waist and clumsily unclasped his holster. He rubbed the palm of his left hand energetically over his face and forehead as if to re-energise himself and pulled out the pistol he had never before held, let alone fired.

Frank, unaware of what was happening behind him, walked to the foot of the stairs he had descended only minutes earlier.

'Get back here. Now!' Stephen had dredged-up from somewhere a previously undiscovered assertiveness as he rose from the bench. Frank put his foot on the first step. 'Stay right where you are. Not one more move. Remember, you're under arrest. This is a final warning.'

Leitch turned to his fellow RP. He spoke gently. 'Put the gun down, son, before somebody gets hurt.'

Frank turned to witness a scene he saw as nothing more than false courage fuelled by Millie Barton's beer. He looked at

Cosgrove and ignored the forceful talk. 'Don't be getting carried away, lad. And, by the way, you're forgetting something; I'm not the enemy.'

'I'm not pretending.' The revolver was steadier now, raised to shoulder height and pointing at the target, Private Frank McGarrity. Cosgrove took a few paces forward until there was only ten feet from the end the weapon's barrel and the man under threat.

Frank turned and raised his head to look towards the top of the long flight of stairs. He could not comprehend that this was anything other than a stunt, a scene from some film. After all, Cosgrove was his most vociferous supporter among the band of brothers of the Pioneer Corps. How had it changed so quickly? Nonetheless, there were many residents of Tipperary who would have agreed with the youngster's revised opinion, that McGarrity was shallow; full of hot air. Stephen Cosgrove now agreed with that assessment.

Frank took a second step on his ascent. His mind was already in the Club Bar and sinking a last refreshing glass of beer.

The crack reverberated around the deserted railway station. The trigger had been pulled, the shot fired. Frank gasped. The pain as the bullet entered his body just below his left shoulder blade was excruciating.

He made a short groaning sound as he dropped to his knees before falling forward, his face smashing against the stairs as if in slow motion. The thud of skull hitting stone was sickeningly audible and blood seeped from his nose, crushed by the impact. Stephen lowered the pistol, slowly. He let it fall at his side and stared at the lifeless man in front of him, as if he had just seen a ghost.

Leitch's mouth fell open. His pallor turned grey in an instant and his bulging, bloodshot eyes told a story of astonishment, shock. He ran towards Frank, praying that all was not lost.

'I warned him.' Stephen's voice trembled. His features fell south and the blood drained from his face. He could not take his eyes off his victim. He was in the grip of anguish and confusion. 'You … you heard me,' he stammered. 'I told him to stop. He was a deserter. That's what he was; a deserter.'

Leitch could not conceive what he had just witnessed. He screamed at Cosgrove to 'shut the fuck up'. He knelt beside the casualty and heaved him over on to his back. 'Frank, Frank.' His distress was palpable, his voice faltering as he lightly slapped the face of the man who, seconds earlier, had been trying to entice him to enjoy one last drink.

Is he still breathing? He must be. Please, don't let him die. 'Stay with me, Frank,' he beseeched. 'Hold on, lad. Hold on. We'll get you to hospital.'

The breathless porter arrived hurriedly. 'Is he ...?'

Frank McGarrity *was* dead. Leitch looked round to see Stephen slump to his knees, weeping uncontrollably. 'I meant to ... it was a warning ... ,' he sobbed.

The eerie silence that fell on platform one was suffocating. All eyes were on the lifeless body draped across the steps. Tears trickled down the face of Bert Leitch; his world had collapsed. In those twelve hours that had heralded the arrival of two regimental policemen, scarred by the ravages of war, they had seen their mission turn to tragedy. Frank McGarrity, the man they were sent to arrest – the 'lost property' of the Pioneer Corps - was gone. He was not the only casualty.

And that was how they captured him, the Wild Colonial Boy.

AUTHOR'S NOTE

While this book does not claim to accurately reconstruct the exact chain of events leading to the fatal shooting of Private John Fitzgerald on May 3, 1941, a tragic event that prompted me to write this story, it is inspired by it.

Indeed, details of what happened to Fitzgerald, replaced in the novel by Frank McGarrity, and the two soldiers sent to arrest him, are sketchy, to say the least.

The story does not set out to be the history of the last days of Fitzgerald, the unfortunate victim of this tragedy, who was swiftly forgotten, lost in the swelter of death statistics such as the world had never before witnessed.

What did he do during his stay? Where did he go? Who did he meet?

We have no answers to those questions which is why events have been imagined for dramatic effect.

The press reportage of the incident and the subsequent court hearings would best be described as discreet, which is perhaps not surprising considering the plight of Britain at the time.

With thousands of people killed every month – in April 1941 alone Britain lost 700,000 tons of merchant shipping through enemy action with great loss of life – the death of one soldier was unlikely to make headline news.

Below are some reports of the court cases in the aftermath of the tragic killing of John Fitzgerald. They tell of the final moments of a chilling tale.

SOLDIER CHARGED
WITH MURDER

An English soldier, Pte Stephen Sheppard (38), Pioneer Corps, appeared in private before Sheriff Macdonald at Dundee charged with murder.

He was committed to prison pending further inquiry.

The charge is a sequel to the death by shooting at Tay Bridge Station on Saturday night of Pte John Fitzgerald (34),

140

Pioneer Corps, 24 Atholl Street, Lochee, who was under detention by an escort.

Two of the party – Pte Sheppard and a lance-corporal – were remitted to the Sheriff from the Police Court yesterday morning on the murder charge. Later the lance-corporal was handed over to the military authorities.

The dead soldier leaves a wife and three children, aged 12, 10 and 8.

*

TAYBRIDGE STATION
MURDER CHARGE
A plea of not guilty was entered at a pleading diet of the High Court in Perth yesterday when Stephen Sheppard was charged with murder.

Trial was fixed for 10th June at the High Court in Dundee.

Sheppard denied that on the 3rd May 1941 at Taybridge Railway Station, Dundee, he assaulted Private John Fitzgerald, 116th Company Pioneer Corps, and discharged a rifle loaded with a ball cartridge, shot him in the chest and did murder him.

Mr R. S. May appeared.

There are nine productions in the case and forty witnesses.

*

SOLDIER FOUND
NOT GUILTY
FIRED, BUT MEANT TO MISS
Stephen Sheppard, 38-year-old private in the Pioneer Corps, stepped from the dock and shook hands with his counsel following a unanimous verdict of not guilty of culpable homicide.

Sheppard also shook hands with an officer witness who had stated he was a very good soldier and with other soldiers who had listened to two days' evidence.

Charges related to a Tay Bridge Station shooting affair on May 3, causing the death of Pte John Fitzgerald (34), 24 Atholl Street, Lochee, a deserter under escort by Sheppard and a lance-corporal.

SERVED IN FRANCE
Sheppard, in evidence, said he volunteered in October 1939 and served in France.

He referred to two public house incidents in which he thought Fitzgerald had tried to escape. Fitzgerald was a plausible sort of fellow, and if you listened to him he could make you believe the moon was made of green cheese.

In the absence of the lance-corporal at the station, Fitzgerald deliberately moved away towards the main street. Witness shouted "Halt or I fire" but there was no reply.

142

He intended to fire past the man's shoulder, but Fitzgerald in keeping moving, made it prove fatal.

Witness denied all three were drunk. He had been ordered to fire if necessary.

To the jury Mr R.H. Sherwood Carver, advocate depute, said the Crown case depended entirely on their taking the view the conduct that night was without any justification whatever and was utterly reckless.

DEMAND FOR
ACQUITTAL
Mr J.G. McIntyre, K. C., asked for full acquittal.

Although there had been a killing, in the absence of a high degree of recklessness there was no crime.

Summing up, Lord Robertson said the jury would keep in view the situation in which the accused was placed. It would be altogether wrong to judge his actions too meticulously. If that were to be done, the actions of soldiers on duty might well be paralysed by fear of consequences, to the greater prejudice of national interests.

Was this shooting in line with the accused's duty as reasonably understood by him, or was it an act, while falling short of murder, that was yet proved to have been of such gross and wicked recklessness that his conduct must properly be regarded as criminal?

The jury returned their verdict after five minutes absence.

*

COURT-MARTIAL
SENTENCE ON N.C.O.
In Charge of Escort in
Tay Bridge Station Tragedy
Finding of the court-martial which followed the fatal shooting of Pte John Fitzgerald, Pioneer Corps, while under escort at Tay Bridge Station on May 3, was promulgated at Dundee yesterday.

Lance-Corporal James Dunlop, who was in charge of the escort, has been sentenced to 156 days' detention.

The charges of which he was found guilty were: (1) That he was unfit for duty owing to previous indulgence in alcohol and (2) that he removed Fitzgerald from the custody of the civil power, improperly allowed him to visit relatives in Dundee, and that he and Private Stephen Sheppard, a member of the escort, and Fitzgerald drank together in public houses.

Two charges on which Dunlop was acquitted were of being drunk while in charge of the escort, and of giving improper orders about firing to Private Sheppard.

Printed in Great Britain
by Amazon

10981254R00088